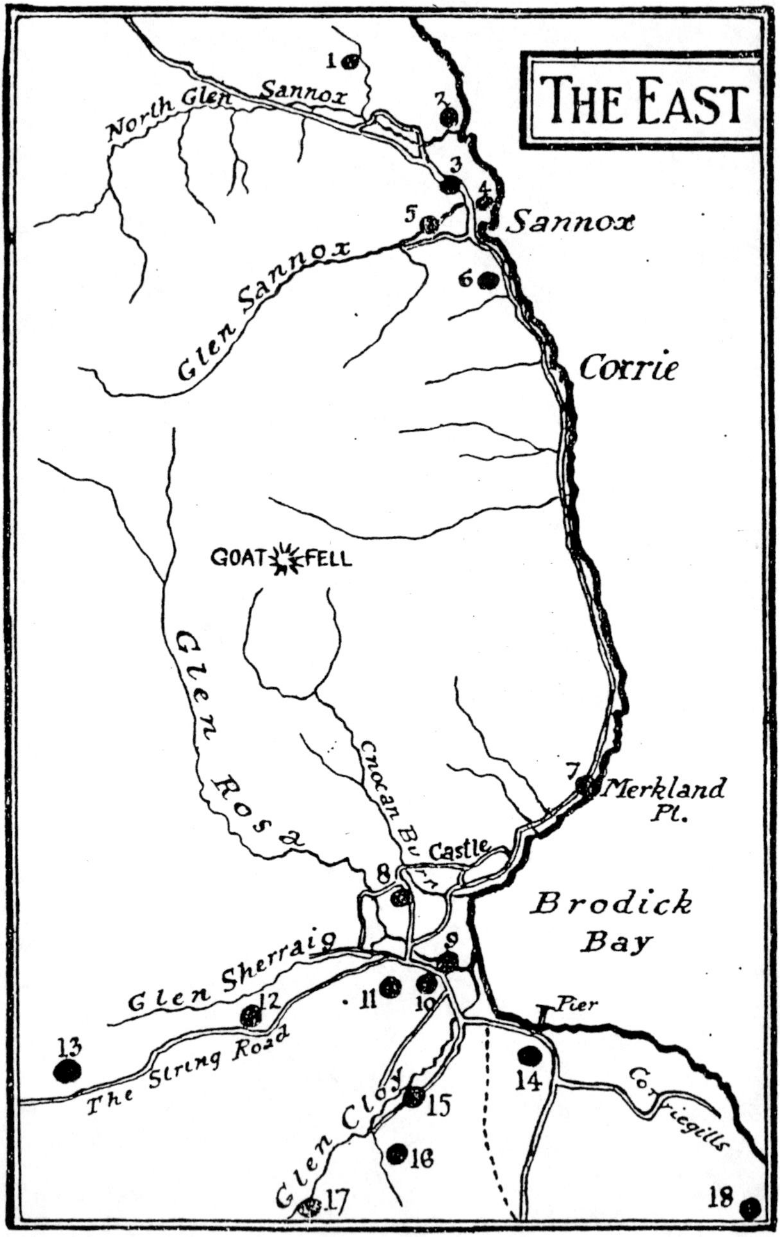
THE EAST
North Glen Sannox
Sannox
Glen Sannox
Corrie
GOAT FELL
Glen Rosa
Cnocan Burn
Castle
Merkland Pt.
Brodick Bay
Pier
Glen Sherraig
The String Road
Glen Cloy
Corriegills
1
2
3
4
5
6
7
8
9
10
11
12
13
14
15
16
17
18

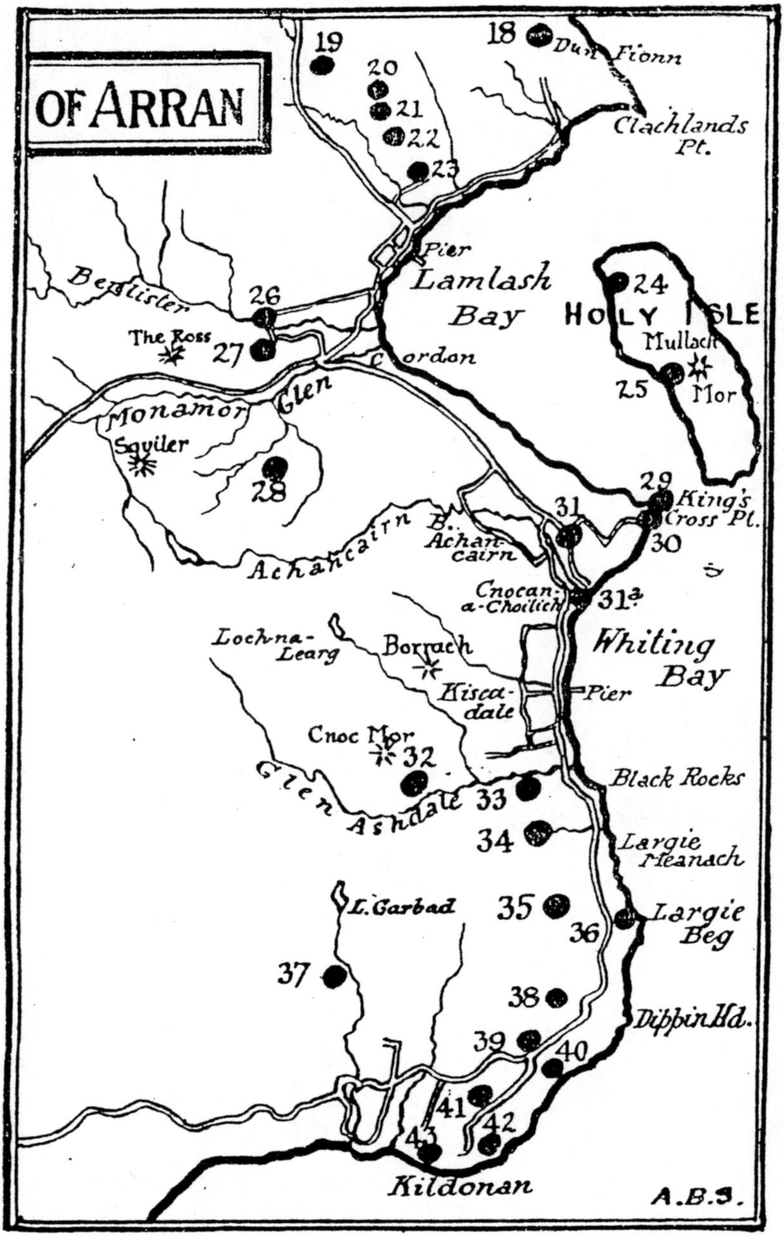
OF ARRAN
19
20
21
22
23
18
Dun Fionn
Clachlands Pt.
Pier
Lamlash Bay
24
HOLY ISLE
Mullach Mor
25
Benlister
26
The Ross
27
Cordon
Monamor Glen
Sgiiler
28
29
King's Cross Pt.
30
31
Achancairn B.
Achancairn
Cnocan-a-Choilich
31a
Whiting Bay
Loch-na-Learg
Borrach
Kiscadale
Pier
Cnoc Mor
32
Glen Ashdale
33
Black Rocks
34
Largie Meanach
35
L. Garbad
Largie Beg
36
37
38
Dippin Hd.
39
40
41
42
43
Kildonan
A.B.S.

THE EAST OF ARRAN

"Set the soles of your feet on my feet, and look!"—P. 204.

THE EAST OF ARRAN

A GUIDE-BOOK FOR THE YOUNG OF ALL AGES

With Stories, Illustrations and a Map

BY

A. BOYD SCOTT, M.C., B.D.

ILLUSTRATED BY DAVID HEYLIN RUDD

PAISLEY: ALEXANDER GARDNER
Publisher by Appointment to the late Queen Victoria
1919

The East of Arran
First Published 1919

This reprint published 1995 by

The Banton Press
Isle of Arran
Scotland.

ISBN: 1 85652 151 6

SECOND IMPRESSION

PRINTED BY ALEXANDER GARDNER PAISLEY

TO

ROLAND, NORMAN AND GLADYS

CONTENTS

LIST OF ILLUSTRATIONS

PREFACE NUMBER ONE

For Potent, Grave, and Reverend Seniors

IN this book an attempt is made to have old Arran live again in the minds and imaginations of young people. From grey stones are gathered little lectures of the neolithic age, which are made as orderly and pleasant as the author can contrive; and the brook of Arran history thereafter is made to turn successive films, which feature ("feature," I believe, is the proper word) successive scenes of life and adventure in the loveliest of our islands. The book has six sections: (1) the first dealing with the Stone Age; then (2) the time of the Dalriadic (Scotic) Kingdom and the wonderful activity of the Celtic monks; (3) the period of the Norse invasions and settlements; (4) the days of Bruce and his passage through Arran; (5) the Arran belief in fairies, and the origin of it; and (6) the period of the sma' still and the revenue cutter. Each of these six sections has two divisions, the one submitting a "Guide" to the relics, topographical and historical, and the other (headed "The Story") offering a tale, based on the period, and doing something to re-construct it, such as may appeal to the saga appetite which obtains in all folk, little and big alike.

The topical references are to the East side of Arran chiefly, but readers at Blackwaterfoot, or Loch Ranza, will find as full an interest in the book as dwellers in Brodick and Whiting Bay. These references are, after all, illustrations simply of histories and conditions which apply to all regions of Arran. Consideration of space and a lesser acquaintance with the West side of the island have limited the author to the coast and country between Sannox and Pladda, in so far as he plays the part of Guide to actual sites.

Antiquarian accuracy has been honestly attempted. Headrick, Bryce, and the two Landsboroughs have been at the writer's one elbow, and, at the other, Mr. MacKenzie MacBride's beautiful book *Arran of the Bens, the Glens, and the Brave*, and the two sumptuous tomes of the Glasgow-Arran Society's *The Book of Arran*. Their contributions, however, have been construed in a mind which for many years now (man and boy) has been actively inquisitive about the island lore—its bays and antres vast, where the dove of the primitive Church and the raven of the sea-kings built successive nests; its hills and cairns hoary with legend; its fringe of little fields, green as a fairy's kirtle, between the dun moor and the blue sea;

its white clachans, with the thatch drawn over their brows, the better to brood on " the silent, vanished races "; its roofless castles and churches, from which a hundred storms have not quite dispelled the lingering incense and the flavour of old wassail.

The book was conceived during a lengthy period of exile on active service in France, with the 51st (Highland) Division, and subsequently with the 9th (Scottish) Division, and it is, in a way, the love-offering of a heart which, with thousands of others, went out to Scotland then, with a passion of devotion and a bairn's love, so articulated and enriched, that we felt we had scarcely known her of old.

PREFACE NUMBER TWO

For Lads and Lasses

THERE are three situations in which you may read this book. The *first* is in Edinburgh, or Glasgow, or Paisley, or Kilmarnock, or in whatever town you live, on through the winter and the spring and the early summer, to the hour when the cab (or it may be a taxi now-a-days) drives up to the door and the luggage is piled up on it, and off you go to the station and the train, and then to the steamer that beats her foaming way across to Brodick or Whiting Bay. When the wintry days grow dark at four o'clock, and the streets are dreary and slushy, and the blinds are drawn, and the fire blinks bonnily, then is a good time to open this book, and read of the summer places, the sandy bays and the heather hills and all, together with the stories that are told about them.

A *second* situation in which to read this book is in Arran itself, sitting on a cushion against a tree, or on a rug against a rock on the sand. Of course, you can do without cushions and rugs altogether if you like. Or, if you can bag a deck-chair, when the old folks have left them, and get it into the shade of the house, or under the big thorn-tree you know at the gable-end, where the fuschia bush is—that's a jolly place to read! And afterwards you may say, "Come on, let's have a hunt for these old graves or old cave" (or whatever it is you've been reading about); "it's just over there!"

But perhaps the *third* situation in which this book may be read is the very best. It is to carry it off to some one of the places mentioned in it, and there read the "Guide" and the "Story" for yourself. Or, if there is a party of you, get some one with a good pronunciation, who can raise his voice at the commas, to read it aloud. A father or an uncle is useful at such a time as this, when he has smoked a cigarette or half a pipe-ful after tea—that is, if it is a picnic, although, to be sure, you don't require to get up a picnic when you go to visit these old places.

If you take the third way, you may want to know the best places in the East of Arran at which to read the different parts of the book. (1) For "The Giants," I would certainly recommend the Giant's Grave[34] at Whiting Bay, or up at the waterfall in Glen Ashdale: but any place you know of with standing stones, or stone circles, or cairns, will do as well. (2) For "The Holy Island," the best place, of course, is on Holy Isle itself, at the Cave—not the cave near the lighthouse, but St. Molaise' Cave,[25] half-way between the lighthouse and the farm. (3) For "The Vikings," the best place is right on King's Cross Point:[29] but Dun Fionn,[18] above Clachlands Point, Lamlash, or the old fort in North Glen Sannox,[1] or, indeed, any of the old forts would do. (4) For "The Bruce," you may choose either Brodick Castle, or the old fort knoll called "Bruce's Castle"[17] in Glencloy, or the Cat Stone at Corrie, or the Stabbing Rock at Merkland, Brodick, or the point at King's Cross. (5) For "The Fairies" you may go almost anywhere, because there used to be fairies everywhere, and perhaps they are still there, who knows! But ask the old people where you are staying, and I am sure they will tell you of a "fairy place" near at hand. If not, go to any of the cairns or old graves, or standing stones, and you will find, as you read that part of the book, that you are right on the spot. (6) For "Ships and Smugglers," the best place is at Largie Beg,[36] but here again, as in the case of the Fairies, you will be close to the tracks of the old ships and the haunts of smugglers almost anywhere, because smugglers at one time were almost as thick as fairies—not *quite* so thick, I should say, but still numerous enough.

As you read the book, you will come across little numerals every now and then stuck above words. These numbers refer to similar numbers dotted over the Map, which you will find inside the covers of the book. The numbers above words in the pages of the book are meant, accordingly, to guide you at once to where the places referred to are to be found. Besides the Map, there is a List (on last page of text) which gives in the *first* column the numbers dotted over the Map, in the *second,* a description of the places they refer to, and, in the *third* column, the chief pages throughout the book in which those places are mentioned.

THE GIANTS: THE GUIDE

THE GIANTS: THE GUIDE

"Grey recumbent tombs of the dead in desert places,
Standing stones on the vacant wine-red moor,
Hills of sheep, and the homes of the silent vanished races."
—R. L. S.

ONCE upon a time there were Giants in Arran. So people say: but most of us now smile at this. They say that the chief of the Giants was called Finn or Fingal, and they tell how he and his sons and clansmen hunted wild beasts in the island and did great deeds. The hill above Clachlands Point, Lamlash, called Dun Fionn [18] was a fort of his. The cave at Blackwaterfoot, which is now known as the King's Cave was once called Fingal's Cave by the people of Arran. In this cave a son was born to Finn. He must have been a fine boy, because a deep mark, two feet long, is shown on the side of the cave which the babe made with one kick of his foot. On the Machrie Moor, there is a circle of standing stones called Finn's Caldron-Rest, because it was on these that he rested his pot to boil it. Finn laid down stepping-stones in the sea between the door of the cave and the coast of Kintyre. By these he would pass over, and, with great strides, walk down to the Mull, and then step over to Ireland by the Giant's Causeway, the remains of which in Ireland are still to be seen. Finn had two sons, called Fergus and Ossian. Both were mighty Giants, great in war and hunting, and skilled in song and playing upon the harp. Of these, Ossian died in Arran, and was buried in what is called Ossian's Grave at Clachaig.

The greatest of their graves is the one high up on the hill-side above the mouth of Glen Ashdale in Whiting Bay.[34] It is certainly long enough for any Giant that one would care to meet. And yet it cannot have been a very comfortable grave, because the length of the grave is divided up by great stones set up in it and across it like the inside walls of a house. They must have cut up the Giant into proper lengths, before they got him snugly stowed away. In truth, however, it is not a Giant's grave at all. It is indeed a grave, or rather it is what we might call a whole cemetery, all crowded together; but it has nothing to do with the Giants of Finn. It has to do with a forgotten people who lived in what is called the later Stone Age, and whose story has been slowly spelled out by wise men in our own day. Let me tell you something of what these wise men have found out about the people who built and used what we call the Giant's Grave, and others like it.

Long, long ago, in that dim age when people went about clothed in the skins of wild beasts, long before bronze or iron were known among men, the people who lived on the shores of the Mediterranean Sea began to move westward and then northward. They were very savage; their weapons were made of stone; their food was got by hunting; they dwelt in caves and underground huts. In appearance they were dark-haired, in height they were neither short nor tall, and their heads were long in shape. No person knows what this race was called, but, because of their long-shaped heads, learned men have given them a name —a name made up of two Greek words, which means "long-headed." These Longheads, then, began to move westward and northward from the Mediterranean. They moved into what is now called Spain, and from Spain they crossed the mountain ranges into France, and then they spread north through France to the narrow sea we call the English Channel. When they reached this strait, the Longheads divided in two directions. One part of them wandered on by the sea-shore, through what is now Belgium, and further still until they had peopled the country as far as the Baltic Sea. The other part managed, somehow or other, to cross the sea to Ireland and settled there. But of those that wandered through Ireland, some crossed over to Scotland, like the spray of a wave, and, like spray, sprinkled themselves on Kintyre and the western islands and on the islands of Arran and Bute.

Well, now, it was these Longheads who built the Giant's Grave. The Giant's Grave was the burial-place of that clan of Longheads who settled in the woods and shore about Glen Ashdale. Let me tell you how they built it. They made a corridor (a part of which you now see) of great flat slabs of stone, which they set up on end, forming two long walls. This corridor they divided into rooms by setting up slabs at intervals across it. Then they placed slabs above the corridor to form a roof. And then they raised a great mound or cairn of stones and earth over it all. But they left room in the cairn to get into one end of the corridor. Here was the door of the clan burial-place they had now made. At the door-end of the cairn or mound they set up tall standing stones in a half-circle which formed a kind of avenue and courtyard to the burial-place; and here, too, they had stones or rocks carved with circles and hollowed like cups, where they placed food and drink for the use, as they thought, of their dead friends within. Very little now remains at the Giant's Grave of all this work. The cairn is gone, although it once was 100 feet long and sixty feet broad; the greater part of the corridor of grave chambers is gone too, the roof has fallen aside, and the standing-stones, with the exception of one, have disappeared. But what you still see was the scene of many cries and tears long ago among those earliest dwellers in Arran, the Long-heads. They carried the dead chief or clansman to the door of the cairn, and into the darkness they drew him, setting him up in a corner of it, with bow and flint arrows beside him, and so left him. Or, as they did in later days, they burned the body first, and then, collecting the bones and ashes in an urn, they placed it in the gloomy chamber. In the year 1902 skilful searchers dug up the Giant's Grave and found burnt bones in it, and arrow-heads made of flint, and broken pieces of pottery.

Besides the Giant's Grave, there are in Arran several other similar burial-places, or cairns with long chambers, which the Longheads made. (1) Another one, though much smaller, is to be seen sixty feet to the south of the Giant's Grave. (2) There is another at Glen Sannox,[6] where burnt bones were found. (3) There are two at Blair-more, Lamlash, called Dunan Beag,[21] and Dunan Mor.[20] Of Dunan Beag two chambers remain, in one of which (the south one) the remains of two bodies were found, which had been buried in a doubled-up position; fragments of pottery and pieces of a jet necklace were also found. Of Dunan Mor three chambers remain; here a flint knife was found. (5) Another is found near

Glenrickard Cottage in Glencloy, Brodick, above Kilmichael House.[16] (6) Another, difficult to find, lies in the high moor, 400 feet up, about a mile south of the Monamor burn;[28] three of its avenue half-circle of standing stones remain. (7) There is another cairn called the Dippin Cairn,[38] on the hill above Dippin, not far from the coast road; it is now a heap of stones, with one wall only of the chambers standing. (8) There are vague remains of a long cairn[4] at the mouth of South Sannox Burn. (9) Cairn[12] on the right of the String Road, Brodick, about one and a half miles from the sea-shore. (10) A mile and a bittock further on and again to the right of the String Road is a "cairn,"[13] but it is not a burial mound. It is called "Columba's Resting-place," and marks the spot where the Saint rested once on a journey across Arran. (11) Chamber at Ballymeanach,[37] on the banks of the burn flowing from Loch Garbad.

All this time I have been telling you of the Longheads. But there still remains to be told another part of the story of those forgotten times. Some time after the Longheads set out on their wanderings, which took some of them to the Baltic Sea, and others of them to Arran, another race of savage white men, far away in Asia this time, became restless and began to wander westward. They spread over what is now called Russia, and, on reaching the North Sea, they passed over to Britain, and settled along the east coast. But their needs and love of wandering urged them westward still; they spread across Britain, and some of them landed in Arran and on the other islands and shores of the Clyde.

Now, who were those people, what was their name, and what were they like? Well, to begin with, we don't know their real name, any more than we know the real name of the Longheads. But these new people had a broad-shaped head, and, because of this, and to distinguish them from the Longheads, wise men have called them also by a name made up of two Greek words, which means "broad-heads." This new people, therefore, we call the Broadheads. They were about the same height as the Longheads, and they were alike, too, in being dark-haired. But they were not so ignorant as the Longheads. They had got beyond the age of stone weapons, and were able to make weapons of bronze. This means that they were a stage further on the way of civilisation than the Longheads, who were dwelling in Arran when they arrived, and you would think that the Broadheads must have made short work of the Longheads. For, of course, they came to blows. The Broadheads wanted Arran for themselves, and the Longheads very properly objected. Thus many a fight occurred in the glens and on the moors and shores of the island between the two races of wild men. The Broadheads did not get it all their own way by any means. Here and there they had victories, and gradually they won places, where they settled firmly, but they did not completely conquer the Longheads. Indeed, it may be said that after the war between them had lasted through many generations, it was the Longheads rather than the Broadheads who remained in possession. But I shall say something more of this presently. Meantime let us hear something more about the Broadheads.

As I have just told you, the Broadheads gained places in Arran, where they settled down to live, hunting, fishing, fighting, bringing up their children in stone and turf houses shaped like beehives, and burying their dead in a way of their own. The Broadheads had their own way of burying their dead. It differed from that of the Longheads, of which you have now learned something. The Broadheads placed their dead in what is called a *cist,* a word which means a box-like chamber, and which is akin to the Scots word "kist." A cist may best be described by saying that it was like a single one of the chambers in the corridor, into which the Longheads' cairn was divided. It was made of flat slabs of stone, floor, sides, and roof, and it was built to hold only a single body. The body was bent up and laid within on its right side.

Sometimes the cist was covered with a mound, or by a cairn of loose stones; sometimes it was surrounded by a circle of tall standing stones. In later days the body was burned, and it was the ashes, gathered in an earthen jar, that were placed in the cist, which was now made smaller than it used to be.

You may want to know where these cists are to be found. Several have been laid bare and examined, but there must be others still, waiting to be discovered, and very many others that have disappeared. The following, however, can be visited. (1) There is a cist near the road between Lamlash and Brodick. It is situated at the centre of a circle [19] of standing stones, which once were seven in number, but of which only four remain. The circle is seventeen feet across, and in the centre of it is a stone flag which covers the cist. In 1861 it was opened, and burnt bones were found. South of the circle, twenty-two yards away, is a single standing stone, four and a half feet high. (2) Cist at Cnocan a Choilich [31a] (Knockankelly, Whiting Bay). In this cist a very beautiful urn was found, richly marked with dog's-tooth pattern, and also the skeleton of a youth. (3) Cist at Glenkil.[27] Here in 1886 a skeleton was found and a broken urn. (4) Achancairn cist.[31] This cist is still complete. It is a small chamber built to receive an urn with burnt bones, which were found when it was opened in 1909. A flint weapon, which had been scorched with fire, was also found. (5) A cist existed at Largie Beg Point, close to the beach in a green mound,[36] on which are still to be seen two standing-stones (two and a half feet above ground) which are all that remains of what was a stone circle. There are also cists at (6) Benlister Burn,[26] Lamlash, and (7) North Sannox,[2] (8) Merkland Point,[7] and (9) Dippin, Greenhill.[39]

"Standing Stones," some of which were probably parts of circles, while others were single monuments above graves, are to be seen at (1) the Deer Park, Brodick,[8] (2) the famous Stronach stone,[9] near Brodick School, (3) East Mayish,[14] between Brodick and Corriegills, (4) near the cairn of Dun Beg, to the left of the road between Brodick and Lamlash,[22] (5) on the hill above Largie Bay,[35] and (6) at Kildonan, west of the hotel.[43]

Perhaps this list of old stones may be tiresome to you. But I put them all in, because, wherever you are in the East of Arran, from Sannox to Dippin, you are staying not far from one or more of these old stones, and so you will be able to go out and see it for yourself, and think of the wild men of old who hunted the deer and fought the wolves and bears, and smote one another with axes and hammers of stone and knives of bronze, in these quiet glens and over these sunny moors where now you make holiday.

I told you how the Longheads were not entirely conquered by the Broadheads. There came a time when the two races mixed with each other. We know this, too, from those old burial-places; because in various places (such as the Giant's Grave [34]) we find that the Broadheads dug out room for their burial cists in the cairns of the Longheads. Thus, in death at least, they made peace with one another. But in life, too, they came to terms, and the Broadheads and the Longheads mingled together. Yet, on the whole, it was the Longheads who got the upper hand, or, as one may put it, got the upper *head*.

THE GIANTS: THE STORY

THE GIANTS: THE STORY

"The Tale of Wolf-fang and Running-Hare"

I

THE sun was slowly lifting the morning mist that filled Glen Ashdale,[32] when old Wolf-fang crept on hands and knees from the tunnel of his house, and, standing upright, gave a shout that sounded more like the bark of a wolf than the cry of a man.

I have called the door of his house a tunnel, for so it was. It was a low, dark corridor which ran far into a great cairn of stones covered with turf. Inside, the corridor ended in a room, with a roof made of great stone slabs, and strewn with the skins of wild beasts. Arrows of wood, tipped with flint, were stuck in the chinks of the walls, and on pegs of wood driven between the stones hung axes with stone heads, lashed with thongs to their wooden hafts. At the head of a rude couch made of deer-skins sloped two stout spears, made as the axes were made. Outside, near the entrance, lay a great round stone, which Wolf-fang at night would tug to himself to fill up the mouth of the passage, lest the wolves should find their way within. Wolf-fang, as he came forth that misty summer morning, could see the marks of their paws around the ashes of the fire at which yesterday's food had been roasted; even the bones had been carried away by the scuffling thieves.

But Wolf-fang had other things to see to as he barked and slapped his hands and shuffled in his furry feet round the house to a neighbouring mound. At last he had an answer to his shouting. Out from the neighbouring cairn came, bounding like a rabbit, a young man, showing his teeth in a grin that was half merriment and half fear. Wolf-fang lifted the spear he carried in his hand and aimed a blow at the lad, which missed. The lad shrieked with laughter, and popped within his house again, as quickly as a rabbit to its burrow, and the old man coughed and turned away. They seemed to understand each other, these two, for presently the lad came out again and passed round to the other's door, where Wolf-fang awaited him, armed for hunting; and, without a word, the two passed beyond the village of mound dwellings, over the rampart of earth and stones, through the trees, and, crossing the warm, flat rocks of the stream, just above the great waterfall, moved upward through the bracken and the heather to the hills.

As they climb in silence through the wet heather,

I may turn aside for a moment to tell you further who they are. The lad is called Running-Hare. He is the son of Grey Raven. But Grey Raven died three months ago, and lies buried in the great cairn we now call the Giant's Grave, leaving the chiefship of this little clan of Longheads to this boy. Wolf-fang has charge of the lad. When Grey Raven fell in the fight at the north end of the bay against the Badger and his men, he called Wolf-fang to him before he died, and, holding his son with one hand, he dipped the other in his own blood and drew it across Wolf-fang's throat, leaving there a broad, red mark. Thus Wolf-fang knew that he must care for Running-Hare to his last breath.

Running-Hare was a ready pupil, quick to learn all the thrusts of the spear and the parries of the axe, quick, too, in setting the arrow to the thong of the bow, clever too at chipping and grinding the flakes of flint into arrow-heads, and swift in the hunt as a hare on the wide moors. As he climbed the hill that morning, with his deer-skin hanging loose beneath his shoulders, his bow and arrows slapping about his back, and his spear darting in playful thrusts at the tufts of heather as he went, he was as brave and blithe a young hero as any of the sons of Finn! His step was as springy as the green and yellow moss through which they plashed from time to time, and old Wolf-fang looked aside at him with pride in his heart, although he would not let it show in look or word.

But now the old warrior and the young chief are well up the high hill-side. They pass the little flint quarry, scooped out of a steep bank like a big buttercup. It is here the best arrow-heads are found and shaped. It is here that old Bear-tusk has his den, the oldest member of the clan. A surly old fellow is he, keeping himself apart from the others, and never talking unless it be to praise the better years that are gone and the braver life of the ancients. He eats his meat raw, and foretells the decay of the world, now that all men roast the good red flesh at fires. But they are all respectful to old Bear-tusk, for his temper is as hot as any fire, and his right arm is as ready as ever to strike, and, besides, there are no arrow-heads so thin and tapering and sharp as his. Round the upper lip of his quarry pass Wolf-fang and Running-Hare, and the ancient man, looking up, lifts high his hand in salute, and as quickly bends down again to his chipping. Wolf-fang pauses to look back over the glen and away along the bay to the point, where Holy Isle lies like a giant otter on its dam. At the mouth of the stream [31a] we now call the Achancairn Burn, several thin columns of smoke rise straight up in the quiet air. Fire burns in Wolf-fang's eyes as he watches the spires of blue reek; he clenches his hand upon his spear; he stamps with both feet on the ground, so that the dew falls in a shower from his wolf-skin.

"Much meat," he mutters, with a snarl that shows his yellow fangs, "much meat and early, the Shore Folk!"

Those are the people, the clan of the Badger, that brought Grey Raven to his death. Although they are all of the one race, there is great hatred between the folk of the Badger and the folk of the Raven. But let Wolf-fang save his hatred for greater foes, because an enemy is making ready to fall upon the island, which will make the feuds of the Longhead clans with one another seem very small affairs!

The two hunters have almost reached the ridge of the high hill, and now they must go warily, for the deer may be grazing just over that pale sky-line. Wolf-fang moves to the right, Running-Hare to the left, and they creep upwards towards the blue sky. As they worm their way through the heather like adders, they know with an instinct which animals have in the hunt, that the living meat is not far away. They make ready arrow and bow, when suddenly a young deer leaps upon the rocky ridge, and, wavering for a moment, bounds between the hunters, and so down the hill and away!

But why did they not shoot? Because both had

seen something! They had seen the shaft of an arrow stuck like a quill in the neck of the hunted beast. So there were other hunters beyond the ridge, not of the Raven folk! And what right had hunters, not of the Raven folk, to be slaying meat on these high moors of the clan? Wolf-fang must see to this! He signs to Running-Hare to join him, and they crawl forward to the rocks that stand up on the ridge like jaggèd teeth, and between the jaggèd teeth they spy out the moor beyond. Their hearts leap with surprise at what they see! A score of men are advancing in a wide half-circle up the hill towards them, such men as they had never seen before. They belonged to none of the Arran clans. Dark-haired men, broad of brow, square of face, clad in bear-skins, armed with spears with blue-green heads, and great green knives at their sides—who could these strangers be? *You* know who they were. They were the first-comers to Arran of the people from far Asia, called the Broadheads.

But Wolf-fang and Running-Hare had no time to consider their origin. All they knew was that a stranger race was in the island, and their blood boiled at the thought. Wolf-fang gnashed his teeth in anger against them, and fingered his bow as though he would fight them there and then. Running-Hare, too, felt an anger like molten fire run up his body to his brain, and, not being so wise as Wolf-fang, he jumped up suddenly on the ridge, and, drawing his war-bow to the full, shouted mightily and let drive the shaft. The strangers halted for a moment, but only for a moment; for, when they saw one of their number fall writhing to the ground, and the proud bowman shouting on the rock, they replied with a fierce yell, and closed in upon the slayer at a run.

With a grasp like the bite of a bear, Wolf-fang drew back the lad, and, barking out quick commands, he leapt with him down the rocks and away down the hill, their pursuers following up the chase like a wolf-pack. But the pursuit was not maintained. The Broadheads were on strange ground, and saw signs of dwellers in the glen and along the bay. So they gave up the chase, speeding the two hunters with a flight of arrows that fell harmless in the bracken, and, shaking their fists as men who intended revenge, they gathered themselves together and disappeared.

II

There was great excitement in the village above Ashdale Fall that day. The older men sat round in the centre of the cairns and debated the business. One by one they spoke in words that would sound to you like grunts, and when the council was over, they rose and began a war-dance in a circle, the older men with slow steps and fierce faces, and bodies doubled as they slouched around, uttering hoarse words and beating spear against axe. The younger men danced with greater spirit, yelling and whooping and waving their weapons wildly about; while the women were the fiercest of all, making horrible grimaces and such gestures as slitting the throats of their enemies, or ripping up the bodies of the slain. Swift scouts had been sent out over the hill, but these, on their return, made signs with their empty hands and said the moors held nothing but birds in their nests and the deer quietly grazing, and so the village became peaceful again, and all went about their ordinary affairs.

That night, as dusk fell and all was still save the sound of the waterfall and the distant calls of wild beasts on the hills, Wolf-fang and Running-Hare left the village. As before, they crossed the stream above the fall, but now they turned to the left, through the tall fir-trees, and so along the steep hill-side that flanks the river to the sea. Besides their clumsy weapons, the one carried a slice of red flesh hanging from a thong about his neck, while the lad carried a leather bottle, which contained the ale those men of long ago made from the flowers of heather. And this they did, because to-night, at moon-rise, it was Running-Hare's duty to take the " food of the dead " to his father's

“Quiet and monstrous big he seemed in the moonlight.”—P. 41.

grave in the burial-cairn of the clan. Thus they travelled in the twilight, through the deep bracken and over the little hollows where the bog mirtle smelt sweet in the dew, and up through the heather, and across the grey grass to the place we call the Giant's Grave.[34]

Very tall and eerie seemed the half-circle of standing stones around the entrance to the cairn. Even Wolf-fang trembled as they drew near. But there was something there besides the silence of the awful stones, to make them pause, and the unseen presence of the dead warriors' ghosts. Alongside one of the pillars stood a man, black and quiet and monstrous big he seemed in the misty moonlight. He saw the others, and quickly and silently as a ghost he flitted behind the tall stone. As quickly and silently Wolf-fang tapped a message on the arm of Running-Hare, and the lad lay down and began creeping away and round to win a position behind the stranger. For a little while nothing was heard. Suddenly from behind the pillar rose the shriek of a man caught fast. Running-Hare was upon him, his nails in the stranger's throat, and the two twisting and buckling on the ground. Swift as an arrow leapt Wolf-fang to the fight. The stranger was beneath, gurgling in his gullet, and trying to free his dirk from the weight of Running-Hare's body upon it. At once Wolf-fang drew a war-arrow and drove the flinty point home in the other's heart, where it snapped asunder. The breast of the stranger heaved once; he sighed, and then collapsed in death.

"Look!" whispered Running-Hare, holding up the dirk. "He is a stranger from the hill."

Such a weapon they had not seen before. It was made of bronze.

The body they dragged beyond the circle of stones. From its breast Wolf-fang stripped a piece of flesh, and this, with the deer-flesh he had brought, he set on the ringed rock at the entrance to the cairn. Running-Hare took of the stranger's blood and mingled it with the heather ale, and poured the mixture into the cup that was hollowed in the rock. They knew that the ghost of Grey Raven would feed that night, proudly and well.

Proud and pleased were the two as they wended their way back again. But Wolf-fang had anxious thoughts as well. Plainly the Broadheads were still close at hand. War would have to be, and who could measure what strength and numbers these strangers with the heavy green weapons might show.

A great shouting up the glen gave a sudden and startling shape to Wolf-fang's brooding thoughts! Then silence, and again a mighty crying from the direction of the village. The attack had come! With a savage word to Running-Hare, Wolf-fang led the way down the hill to the river. They dared not go back the way they had come, for by now the enemy must be over the stream above the Falls. So well below the Falls they crossed, and up the other side, through the birch-trees and the hazels they hurried, with breasts that seemed ready to burst for breath. Louder and louder still came the shouting in the high glen. But they knew that these were not yet the cries of men in mortal fight with one another: nor could they make out the blood-curling shrieks which the women make when they join in battle.

III

The assault on the village was just about to be made, when Wolf-fang and Running-Hare climbed over the great rampart, and leapt down among the clan. It was clear that the Raven folk were far outnumbered. It was clear, too, that destruction and death were in store for them all, unless assistance could be had. It was this that the chief men were discussing when Wolf-fang and Running-Hare arrived. They shouted in joy when they saw them, and at once Running-Hare was hailed as the one who should fly for help. Was he not the outstripper of the brown hare herself for speed? Away! let him speed for the life of the clan!

Away with him! let him fly to the folk of the Dark Eagle and the folk of the Sleeping Weasel, and beseech them to come, and quickly to come!

Off sped Running-Hare. The village was rattling with the arrows of the enemy, and the first wave of their attack was struggling on the western side of the rampart, as the lad climbed over the eastern wall, and took to the lonely path over the misty moor. Up past the great ravine we call the Devil's Cauldron, up through the pools of black peat on the topmost moor, along the shore of Loch na Learg he ran, straight as a hare, lithe and free as the red deer. His heart did bump indeed as he ran along the shore of Loch na Learg; but the great monster, which inhabits the loch, with the skin of a seal and the bill of a sea-goose, remained undisturbed. Along the little track, which still goes like a white thread through the peat and heather, he ran, and so down the hill to the shore at the mouth of Monamor Burn. Here lay the village of Dark Eagle's clan.

Loudly shouted Running-Hare, and out came the shaggy Eagle people. All panting, Running-Hare told his tale, making eager signs when words failed him for lack of breath. And eagerly the kinsmen of his clan responded. First of all they sent off their swiftest runner to the folk of the Sleeping Weasel, whose village lay in Glencloy on the green grass levels near the shore. And then the warriors of Dark Eagle filed out of their village, very much as Red Indians do when going on the war-path. Their chief began to run, with Running-Hare ahead of him, the others took up the pace, and thus running and leaping they breasted the hill and swung their way across the moor. Beside the chief ran his two tame wolves, ferocious beasts, with skin as thick as the pelt of bears, and teeth like the fangs of lions.

On nearing the scene of the fight at Glen Ashdale, they swung to the right, and struck the stream well above the village. Down the river they came, with the purpose of taking the enemy in the rear, one hundred and ten men, fleet of foot, and strong as the wild boars of their own glen, loosening their weapons to their hand as they followed their leader to the place of murderous cries.

Not a moment too soon was their coming. Some of the strangers had gained a footing within the rampart. Already the others were massing upon the dyke for the final assault, when the clan of the Eagle fell upon them and got busily to work, with the shrieks that great birds make, fighting to defend their nests.

"Grey Raven! Grey Raven!" cried Running-Hare as he charged, and his people within knew that help had come, and rallied with an answering call and a foray that cleared the village of the invaders. Caught between two packs, fiercer than winter wolves, the Broadheads gave way. Some fled up the stream, and so won off to the hill. But a score of them or more were surrounded as they tried to cross the river above the Fall. The folk of Dark Eagle had them held on the southern bank, the folk of the Raven on the northern side, and Wolf-fang and Running-Hare and the chief of the Eagles came upon them down the channel of the river. Behind them was the great waterfall! There was no escape. But a chief of the strangers, mighty in stature, armed with a great bronze sword, and carrying a round shield made of ox-hide, and studded with bronze nails, stood bravely forward to hew a path of escape for himself and his clansmen. He had not gone three paces, when out from the group about Wolf-fang leapt the two great wolves of the Eagle. The stranger chief struck with his sword and smote the head of the one well-nigh in twain. But the other had the tall warrior by the throat, and down they fell together. Straightway, club and axe and spear followed the attack of the wolf, and step by step the band of Broadheads was driven backward to the fatal edge of the Falls. The great smooth rocks grew slippery with blood. Blow for blow they gave, thrust for thrust, but all their struggle was in vain. With a great shout, the Ravens and the Eagles made a final charge, and the survivors of the enemy were driven over the watery cliff. Into the deep pool they fell and died, and the eels in after days made an end of them.

Thus fared the folk of Grey Raven against the strangers from over-seas. Three weeks afterwards, the Broadheads seized the village of the Badger, and slew all his people, man, woman, and child; and for many days Broadheads dwelt at Achancairn, and for many days the Grey Ravens remained strong and safe in Glen Ashdale above the Falls.

THE HOLY ISLAND: THE GUIDE

THE HOLY ISLAND: THE GUIDE

At times kneeling to Beloved Heaven,
At times at psalm-singing,
At times contemplating the King of Heaven
Holy the Chief,
At times at work without compulsion
This would be delightful.
At times plucking dulse from the rocks,
At times fishing,
At times giving food to the poor.

—SONG OF ST. COLUMBA.

LET us take a boat at Lamlash Old Pier and row across to the Holy Isle. We land at the little quay below the farm.

Now, in making this short voyage, we have done a very extraordinary thing. In leaving Lamlash we have left what is not really Lamlash at all, and, in reaching Holy Isle, we have really reached Lamlash. "Which is absurd!" you say, in the words of the Greek gentleman who built the *Pons Asinorum*. But hold on a moment till I read you my riddle!

Long, long ago, a Christian Saint took up his abode in this little island. While he lived there, and his disciples, the little island was a much more important place than the village we call Lamlash, which was then only a few huts clustered on the shore and up the glen where the road to Brodick begins. The little island was truly a holy island, and came to be called Eilean Molaise after the Saint, that is, " Island of Molaise." For hundreds of years the people called Holy Isle by that name—Eilean Molaise. But the dwellings across the loch, on the mainland of Arran, grew in number and importance, church buildings which once stood beside the farm on the Isle fell into ruin, and people became forgetful of the Saint and his settlement on the little island. The words Eilean Molaise lingered in memory, but the words got shortened and run together, like this—Lan Molaise, then Lanmolash, and then Lamlash, and this word came to be applied to the *village* on the mainland, while the real Eilean Molaise came to be called simply Holy Isle. People hereabouts who speak Gaelic still refer to Holy Isle as Eilean Molaise; and when they speak of going to Lamlash they say they go to Loch-an-Eilean, which means Loch of the Island. It may seem funny to call a village a " loch " like that, but it is just the same as calling the village in the north of Arran Loch Ranza. Thus you see it is not quite so silly as at first it sounded, when I said that in rowing from Lamlash to Holy Isle, we have left what is not really Lamlash at all, and that in reaching Holy Isle we have really reached Lamlash.

But now that we have indeed reached Eilean Molaise, let us take a walk by the shore track, and see what we can see. At first there is not much to delay us. And yet along this shore, past the farm, the ground hides many old and romantic stories. Once upon a time a fortified tower stood there where the corn now grows. It was built 700 years ago, and helped, together with a castle (Lamlash Castle), which stood within the grounds of Whitehouse, to guard the anchorage which Lamlash loch has been from the earliest times. Above the field and against the cliff are still to be seen the remains of red sandstone walls.[24] It is thought that this is all that remains of a church which "friars" built in the fourteenth century. There can be little doubt that sacred buildings of one kind and another have stood here since the days of St. Molaise, and that is twelve hundred years ago. Probably on this spot the Saint and his disciples had their little village of huts, made of wood and turf, with a larger oblong hut which was their church, the whole surrounded by a rampart made of stones and earth, called a *cashel,* and having within it a tall round tower of stone, to which they could retreat in times of danger. At any rate, the spot has always been holy ground. Long after the last of the church buildings had become ruinous, the people from Lamlash and around Lamlash ferried their dead across the loch to bury them in this sweet place. But that custom died one day years ago, when a funeral boat was swamped and several persons drowned. After that they sought out the present burial-ground at Lamlash, and they say that they were guided in their search for a new God's-acre by a light which appeared and led them on to find it.

As we continue our way by the shore track, we pass a cave in the steep hill-side (300 yards distant from the farm) which is called the Smugglers' Cave. I shall tell you of the smugglers another time: to-day we are chiefly occupied in following in the footsteps of the Saint, who made this island sacred. Many a time he must have walked along this very track between the high mass of the hill and the deep sea, as he journeyed to and fro from the huts near the farm to his cave. It is to his cave [25] we are now going. It is to be found half-way between the farm and the lighthouse, midway also along the narrow bay which takes a bite out of this side of the island. The cave is twenty-five feet above the level of the track, but can be detected quite readily, a low, black slit it looks from the shore. You will be sure you have spotted it when you see beside you, immediately to the left of the shore-track, a great rock seven feet high. It is almost round, but the top is flat as a table, with four seats cut out at the corners. On the north side of the rock steps have been cut, by which one may climb easily to the top. On the east face a cross has been carved, having a ring top, and, if you look carefully, other little crosses can be found. These were made by pilgrims who visited the holy place. Now-a-days people call the rock " St. Molaise' Table "; I have heard it called also " St. Molaise' Pulpit "; but the proper name of it is the Judgment Stone. What judgments were made here we can only guess, but probably it was at this stone that the chief of the Church in the island settled disputes among the people, who looked up to him as their father in goodness and justice. Possibly in savage times, before the messengers of Christ came there at all, the stone was the scene of justice among the Stone Age people, and barbarous executions, it may be even of human sacrifice.

Close to the Judgment Stone is seen the Well of St. Molaise. It is not so very long ago that people, with various ailments, stopped coming to this little well in the belief that, as the blessing of the Saint dwelt in its crystal water, it had power to cure them of their complaint.

But now it is time to climb up to the cave itself. A flight of seven rough steps brings us to the entrance. The cave is about forty feet long and thirteen feet broad at its widest part. The floor to the left of the entrance, that is the north end of the cave, is paved. In this part, on the sea-ward side, is a large stone which was probably used simply as a table, although some believe it is an altar stone. Some years ago, when a careful digging was made in the south end of the cave, and the rubbish examined, it was discovered that here was the kitchen of the cave. The black refuse contained limpet and oyster shells, and the bones of oxen, sheep, pig, and deer, some of which had been split to get at the marrow. A fire-place is built in the south wall of the cave. Formerly the fire-place had uprights fixed to the wall, with a flat stone above, but these have collapsed. The sea-ward side of the cave in the time it was in use, was built up by a wall of stones which reached the overhanging rock. Only a part of this front wall is now standing. On the rock face which forms the east wall of the cave can be traced crosses, some of them very ancient, and several of those Norse letters called " runes," thin upright scratches, with cross scratches at intervals. What these mean we shall see when we come later to learn about the Vikings and their visits to Arran.

Let us remain a little longer in this cave or cell of St. Molaise, while I tell you what is known of the blessed man himself. Or perhaps we might go down and rest in the sunshine on the short green turf between the well and the Judgment Stone, for it grows chilly in the cave, and there I shall give you the story. But, first, you must let me trouble you with a little bit of ancient history, in order that we may get the Saint properly into the picture of his time.

About the year A.D. 400, a Gaelic chief called Riada came from Ireland with a band of followers and settled in Kintyre. Others followed, especially a great inflow of settlers under the three sons of Erc, whose names are Fergus, Loarn, and Angus. These clans set up little kingdoms throughout Kintyre and the neighbouring coasts and islands, including Arran; they reached as far north as Mull. From the name of the chief Riada, they are called the Dal-riadic Kingdom. They were the "Scots" who in the end provided the name, though they did not provide all the people, of the land we now know so proudly as Scotland. But that is another story.

Now these Dalriadic people were Christians. Their ministers were monks who lived in little villages of huts by themselves, some of them doing farm work for the brotherhood, some of them making copies of the Scriptures, others conducting the wonderful schools which they started, and all of them living a life of worship and good deeds. These good men followed up their countrymen in Kintyre and Arran and elsewhere in their new settlements, to keep them true to their religion and also to make Christians of the folk, Celtic like themselves, in whose lands they settled as lords. The greatest of these missionary monks was, of course, St. Columba. His cousin, King Connal, whose capital was at Crinan, agreed to Columba's going to Iona, and there the Saint of Scotland built the monastery from which he worked eastward and northward among the wild people called the Picts, whose king, Brude, had his fort where Inverness now stands. Another of these brave saints, called Donnan, founded a church at Kildonan in Arran. He was martyred in the island of Eigg in the year 617. Another founded his monastery on the west coast of Arran on the "Speckled Hill" at Kilpatrick. A few years ago the remains of its round tower and its rampart, or *cashel,* were unearthed. This was the church of St. Brendan (Kil-brendan) which gives the name to Kilbrannan Sound. Another sacred settlement may have been placed at Clachaig, in the south of Arran, of which St. Molaise was founder; old stories tell of St. Molaise going regularly to Clachaig from Holy Isle and resting at a point on the summit of the Ross road called Cnoc na Croise.

And now we are back again to St. Molaise. Just as St. Columba took up his abode on a little island near the mainland, so did Molaise settle on Holy Isle. The name of the Saint is made up of two words, *mo* or *ma* and *Las* or *Lais*. The word *Lais* means "a flame." The word *mo* or *ma* means "my," used in a loving way: it is the same as the middle syllable in the name of Kilmacolm village, which means "Church of the dear Colm (Columba)." Thus Molaise means "the dear Lais" or "the dear Flame of fire." Such, indeed, our Saint was, a shining light of God in those dark ages, and a fire to burn wickedness out of the savage hearts of men.

Molaise was of kingly origin. His grandfather was Aidan, King of Dalriada. King Aidan had fled to Ireland from Dalriada on the death of his father in battle against the Picts, and there his daughter Gemma was born. Gemma married a royal chief called Cairell, and to them was born Molaise. King Aidan, when he returned to Dalriada, brought Gemma and Molaise with him, and there in the king's house the little lad was brought up. His uncle was St. Blane, founder of the city of Dunblane, who ruled a monastery in Bute (St. Blane's Chapel). St. Blane came to see the little Molaise, led by many reports that this was a wondrous child. Wonderful stories, truly, are told of him. While on this visit, St. Blane had one of his horses stolen, but the child pondered and prayed about the theft so strongly, that the thief thought he was pursued by soldiers, and returned to confess his crime. Once (so they say) a man, blind from birth, washed in the water in which the child had been bathed, and lo!

straightway he was cured. And once, in Ireland, when the monastery was attacked by pirates, so earnestly did the young Molaise pray throughout the night, that in the morning, the evil men saw as it were the plain filled with warriors, and they fled in terror. Of this, at least, we are sure, that, as a lad, Molaise was sent by the King to Ireland, to the famous school of St. Fintan there, and so famous he became and beloved, that before he was twenty, the people desired to make him a king. But Molaise would not. Instead of a king's banner, he chose the staff of a missionary monk, and, as the old history says, betook himself to "a certain island of the sea between Britain and Alba," which is Arran, and there he set himself to win subjects for Him who is the King of kings. Thus he came to Holy Isle, living in the cave above us there, and then, I doubt not, as disciples gathered to him, building his village further along the shore where the level ground is. Thus for long he dwelt here, and won a holy kingdom all about these shores.

In after days he went back to Ireland, and became Abbot of Leithglinn in Leinster, and did great works there to the day of his death, April 18, 639. An old song thus sings of him:

> "Blessed Molaise, flame of fire,
> Singing with his comely choir,
> Rath-gil's Abbot, king of flame,
> Son of Monad's lady Gem."

At the beginning of this talk, I spoke of the church which Friars, of a later time, built near the present farm. Just let me add a word here about the other churches in the East of Arran which were built in the Middle Ages. Before the Middle Ages the churches of St. Columba's time and St. Molaise' had been swallowed by the Roman Catholic Church, which spread in great power over all Scotland, and Arran was divided into parishes, as happened throughout the land. At first Arran was one parish with its chief church at Kilbride, Lamlash. Then the southerly part of the island was made into a separate parish with its chief church at Kilmorie.

The ruins of Kilbride Church [23] are still to be seen. It was built in the fourteenth century, and was named after St. Bride or Brigit, the famous abbess of Kildare in Ireland. Built into the east gable is a slab with a crown at the top, a monogram and date (1618) in the centre, and the words "Fir God" (Fear God) at the foot. The letters of the monogram, with the words filled in, of which these letters are the initials, stand for the following: I (James) M H (Marquis of Hamilton) E A (Earl of Arran) D C (Duke of Chatelherault). Among the old sculptured stones, the following may be noted: (1) Stone with head broken off, showing a knight in quilted coat; this is probably the grave stone of the Earl of Arran who died in 1609.

(2) Slab stone with a cross and sword alongside, and rope-work decoration round the edge. (3) Slab stone with shield, outstretched hand, and sword. (4) Stone with shield with bar across it and letters J H and E W. (5) Stone with following inscription round: "Hre lyes Patrick Hamiltoun in Cordan who departed this present life the 15 day of Aprile the yeare of God 1676." In this old graveyard there was found a sculptured cross, which has been set up in front of the present parish church. The front of it shows our crucified Lord passing bodily into a Communion cup. Around His head is an aureole or crown, with a star on either side. From the cup there flows to a figure kneeling at the foot, the healing stream of Christ. On either side of Him is the tree of life. The back of the cross shows a square with a diamond design inside, and within the diamond a star. Some think that this cross stood originally at the monastery on Holy Isle.

Of the first parish church of Kilmorie (which means the church of St. Mary) there is no trace whatever. Indeed the opinion is held by some that it is to be looked for, not at the present parish church, but over the hill at Slidderie, at a spot known as "St. Mary's Chapel." But this is taking us away from the East of Arran.

At Whiting Bay, in Glen Ashdale, there are the ruins of an ancient chapel,[33] but little of it now appears above ground.

In Glencloy, too, there stood once an ancient church,[15] Kilmichael, named after the Archangel.

In Sannox, graves now cover the site of an ancient chapel.[5] But there is an interesting sculptured stone built into the outside of the churchyard wall, which shows an effigy of St. Michael, after whom this church also was named.

THE HOLY ISLAND: THE STORY

THE HOLY ISLAND: THE STORY

"The Tale of St. Molaise and Neil"

I

AS the blessed Abbot Molaise came through the gate in the dyke that encircled the huts of the monastery [24] (on Holy Isle) and stood on the turf above the shore, his eyes were full of peace and his heart glowed with thankfulness to God. Within his breast was calm, and a great calm rested on land and sea and sky. Beyond the purple mass of Goatfell the sun had set, going down in a blaze of rose, while high up and overhead the sky was green and blue as an opal is. The sea lay as in a dream, and the sound of its lazy ripple on the shore was like a sleeper's breathing, hushed and slow. Across the water, strings of smoke went directly up from the group of thatched huts in the shallow valley through which the Brodick road now runs, and in the glen of Monamor, too, the fires of the evening meal were sending up their grey signals. A dog barked, and his clear note startled a heron on the shore of Holy

Isle, so near it sounded. Like a grey gauze the evening mist began to enfold the brown bosom of the hills, but the brow of Mullach Mor, as the hill of Holy Isle is called, still blushed with the sun's parting salute.

Abbot Molaise lifted his eyes to heaven, and he spake a hymn of praise in his heart. He had just come from the church, where the other monks and he had been singing the evening psalms. It seemed to him that God had answered their prayers and holy songs by laying on sea and hill this harmony of colour and calm, and yonder star in the western sky seemed an answering candle to those which the good brothers had lighted on their altar within. Molaise turned round and gazed in love on his dear monastery within its *cashel*. The cellarer was laughing pleasantly at some tale told him by the brothers who had been making hay that afternoon. The scribe Cormag had carried his table out of doors, and was bent over it with great earnestness, fearful of losing a single ray of daylight as he copied on a creamy page of lambskin the beautiful brave Irish letters of the Gospel. In at the Monastery gate passed Fearmur the cowherd, carrying his pails full of foaming milk. His way brought him close by Molaise, and he set down his pails at the Abbot's feet, and knelt to him, to receive a blessing on himself and on the yield of his meek cows, tethered yonder on the grass along the shore. Molaise made the sign of the Cross above the herd-laddie and his pails, and said:

"What spell out of far Manusmor" (it was out of Manusmor in Ireland that Fearmur came) "What spell out of far Manusmor do you sing at the milking of the Lady Gemma and the Lady Lora and the Lady Deirdre, that thy pails burst like this?"—By these names Fearmur called his cows.

And Fearmur blushed with joy, that the blessed man should remember their names, but answered nothing; for he knew that it was by the love that lay between these dumb cattle and himself that the milk was blest and increased. So Fearmur lifted his pails and passed within, his heart glowing with love for the Father Abbot, as an altar shines with light. All the disciples of Molaise and all the servants of God in that age had a wonderful affection for animals and birds, both wild and tame.

Then Molaise called in a voice that sounded far and clear, although he called easily and quietly:

"Little Neil, come hither to me!"

At once, from the door of the church came a young man, tall and straight, and moving with the ripple and grace that a young stag shows as he walks the high hill. He came to the Abbot, and he, laying his hand upon his shoulder, said:

"You will be going with me to the cave,[25] for there I watch and pray this livelong night."

So the two went together by the track along the shore, past Fearmur's three lady cows, until they came to the cornfield. Then Molaise, who had kept silence till now, stopped Neil with his hand and regarded the corn. The field was still green, but there was even then a sprinkle of gold in it and the promise of harvest.

"The harvest will be plenteous, little Neil," said Molaise at last, "and for this we have sicklemen enough. But I pray God to be sending me harvesters and more for yonder ripe fields," he added, pointing to the other shore.

By this he meant the gathering of men and women into the Barn of Christ's Redemption, like sheaves of corn, pure and bright as gold.

"Blessed be God, the lord of the harvest," said he, speaking again, "for He has been sending you to me last night!"

"I cannot speak," replied Neil, "for the tears are in my throat. O, holy father, I have sipped of the water of heaven in thy house, and I have begun to understand the puzzle of Eternity, for lo, this one day hath been to me as a thousand years!"

Molaise smiled lovingly when the lad said this. He was pleased with the love and wisdom of his speech, and a new flame leaped in the Abbot's heart of hope for the monastery in after days. And he did well to have this hope, for, long years afterwards, when Molaise had gone back to Ireland and was dead, Neil became Abbot in Eilean Molaise of Arran, and so great and blessed a man was he that the monks had a proverb which was this: "Like as Molaise and Neil."

Neil had come to Holy Isle the night before, to be made a monk by Molaise. A ship carried him from Ireland to the west of Arran, to the monastery of St. Brendan, and there he had lodged three days. But he would not abide there, for he sought Molaise, since Molaise was kin to Neil's family in Ireland over the sea.

"Speak to me now," said Molaise, as they continued their way along the shore. "Speak to me now and say if the name of the man is known that slew your father and your mother, those dear ones of my own soul, and likewise Cailtan your brother, and the Lady Aethne, your little sister, those children of my heart."

"My lord," replied Neil, "the murderer's name is known of none. He came with his pirate company suddenly one night of this same month of July, four years ago, and when they had done their evil work, they robbed the dead, and pillaged the houses and burned them, and so made away. We had only one man with wounds slight enough to let him carry the news to the Lord Baitan beyond the hill, and to stir him for Christ's sake to the chase of the pirates. Thus they made a long start and got off to the sea, and, as we heard, to three ships which they had. But, holy father," continued Neil after a time, for the Abbot remained silent. "I saw this pirate chief so near that still in my dreams I behold his face. I was a little lad of eleven years then——"

"That makes thine age fifteen now," interrupted Molaise. "Thou hast taken little time to grow that man's body of thine!"

"Pray for me," replied Neil, "that I may grow in holy wisdom as in stature!"

At this the blessed man was again well pleased, for it was these words among others that he had read that morning to Neil out of the Holy Gospel, as touching God's holy child Jesus. But he only said: "So his face comes before thee still in dreams, my son?"

"Yea, father," answered Neil; "I was so young then that I had not courage to come from under the cloak that was thrown on me, when the wild men leapt upon us to slay us. But from beneath the cloak I looked and beheld his face as he stamped upon my dead father's face, and I saw the holy Abbot Artbrannan rush forward and the pirate slay him with his red sword, and I heard Artbrannan cry as he died, 'As a beast of

"He cursed the Saint and blasphemed God."—P. 73.

the sea is clubbed, so will men club thee, thou monster from the sea!'"

Neil could speak no further for weeping at the remembrance of these things. So Molaise spake comforting words to him, and the lad's spirit grew strong and bright again. They stood together now by the Judgment Stone on the shore, beneath the cave in which Molaise had dwelt when first he came to his island, and to which he was wont to pass from the monastery as to a desert place for prayer and thought and fresh resolves.

The night was close at hand, but there was still a silvery light upon the sea, and in its lustre they saw a boat pass close to the shore. It was made of a wooden frame covered with hides, for such were the boats that ancient people used, and it went along without noise save the splash of the oars. But the men in her spied Molaise and the lad on the shore, for he that sat in the stern rose up, and, lifting his fist on high, cried:

"O, Molaise, flame of fire, may the fire of perdition burn thy beard, thou plague of all Arran!"

And with many other and worse words he cursed the saint and blasphemed God, mocking the monks and shouting, "Will I be after bringing a sweet young seal to fill your lean bellies in the morning?" and with this he laughed, and yelling a curse again, he bade his men bend to their oars, and away they went.

Neil felt a flood of hot rage rush through his heart, as he listened to these insults, but there was no sign of anger in the face or voice of the Abbot when he said to Neil:

"Will you see the grey heron standing still in the quiet water there?"

Neil looked and saw the bird dimly in the twilight; he was in the water's edge between them and where the boat had been. Molaise continued:

"The timid bird has not moved at the shafts of those vile words. And shall we, who have the whole armour of God upon us, permit ourselves to be wounded? There goes the vagabond who lurks in Monamor and nightly robs the monastery. For he passes to the rocks behind the south end of our island, where the seals dwell, and slays the meat that the Lord Finn Mac Rydderch gave to my monks and me."

Neil caught a breath of bitterness in the blessed man's voice as he finished, and Molaise felt the breath of it in his own heart, for he shook himself and said:

"Enough! Enough for the day is the evil of it. I will now take the wings of the grey heron and rise to my nest in the cave and there be at rest."

So saying, he gave a blessing to the lad as he

knelt before him, and climbed up to the cave. And Neil returned to the monastery, regretting a little that he was already almost a monk, for his fingers itched to take a sword and seek out the accuser of his brethren, the tormentor of Molaise his father in God.

II

Next morning Neil was awakened by the tinkle of the little bell in the Abbot's hand, and in a trice he was up from the sweet layer of red bracken leaves he called his bed, and the stone he called his pillow, and off to the church for the morning psalms. Great was the singing of the brothers in their brown robes, as the Abbot and they that were with him on his side uttered a verse, and Brother Scanlan and those on his side replied with the verse that followed. And the Abbot prayed and took bread and wine and fulfilled the sacred mystery of Christ's Body and Blood, and in the silence the wash of the waves on the shore sounded like the rustle of wings bringing helpers to the altar.

Thereafter they breakfasted. Porridge of oats and milk from Fearmur's cows, with the cream of it poured secretly into the Abbot's wooden bowl, formed their meal; but, that morning being the anniversary of the blessed man's coming to the island and the founding of the monastery, the cellarer had twelve great trout which a fisherman from Glen Rosa had brought as a gift last night to the monks, and he now carried the steaming dish of them to Molaise, and he, pretending to frown at first, blessed the dish and bade them be given round. At this all the brothers rejoiced, and great talk arose about the ways of trout, and the best pools in Arran, and the older monks had tales to tell of fish they had killed, whereof there were no witnesses save themselves! And so with happy laughter the meal ended, and the Abbot gave thanks and dismissed them all to their several duties. Some betook themselves to the little fields, others to the making of books, and Baitan got him his chisels and betook himself to carve the twisted snakes on the white cross the monks desired to have set up on the other shore, where their brother Colgu had been slain by a wild pirate from Bute two years before.

The Abbot called Neil to him, and the two, carrying down the Abbot's little boat to the sea, got aboard and turned her blunt nose towards the other shore, Neil handling the oars with a strength that drove her snoring through the water. Several from the village gathered in a cluster about them as they landed, eager to be porters of the boat, hailing the Abbot as Father, bending to his blessing, and beseeching him to tarry among them with Gospel words. But Molaise had other business on hand, he told them, and must get to Monamor. When he said this, the people fell silent, and looked aside at one another, and then, with one voice, they cried out that since their old chief died and the young chief had gone to Crinan to the King, the nameless man in Monamor and his blasphemous crew had exceeded all bounds in their pride and evil deeds, and they prayed the Saint to break him! The Abbot answered nothing; so, before he parted from them, one brought his bow and arrows to be blest, for he was going that day to the hill to hunt, and, among others, a woman brought a shuttle from her loom, and a fisherman laid a torn net before the Abbot and besought a spell from God.

To all the blessed man replied, very patiently and shrewdly. To the fisherman he said:

"Mend it with prayer and twine! And, in twining it with prayer and in praying for it with good twine, forget not to break a bottle in sacrifice on the stones beside it!"

At this the people laughed, and the man sulked a little, for he was on the way to be a drunkard. But when the monk placed a hand on his shoulder, his face cleared and, with resolve, he said:

"By the God of Molaise, this thing I will do!"

The Abbot and Neil now betook themselves along the shore by a track which ran where the shore road now runs past the pier and the Row, and then slanting to the right towards the mill of Monamor. It was on the hill-side above the mill we know, and deep in a clearing of the wood which was then dense and great, that the Nameless One and his fellows had their den. Down below, upon the stream, and near the cluster of houses we call Cordan, there dwelt in their turf houses a little clan who suffered much from the evil men above them. To these Molaise turned aside with Neil to see how they fared. Flocking around him with joyful signs and words, they also began to complain of the things they suffered at the robbers' hands. A poor woman led forward a little lad, whose ears had been cut off by the villains for naught else than this, that he had snared a rabbit in the glen beyond their fort. The wounds were still raw, and the woman, making her finger red in them, drew it down the Abbot's robe and cried:

"By blood alone can this blood be washed from thee, thou bard of God!"

The Saint touched the two sides of the boy's head, and, behold, straightway they ceased to bleed. Then, bidding them all have hope in the judgments of God, he lifted his hands in blessing, and left them.

It was clear to Neil that the Abbot was going to do battle with the villains in Monamor. They carried no weapons indeed, but the countenance of Molaise was set as a king's is when he clanks in arms across the fields to war. The day was hot and drowsy, and they went slowly in the scent of the myrtle and meadowsweet and whin, from which the dew was rising in throbs of heat. Neil became suddenly aware that a prince in war array and an aged monk were walking ahead of them by the river path. He blinked his eyes and looked again, and certainly the two strangers were still ahead of them. Whence they had come he could not guess, but his heart smote against his breast when he saw that the prince was his own father, and the monk the Abbot Artbrannan! He turned in amazement to Molaise, but the look on the face of the kingly Abbot was that of a man who is far out of hearing, and he muttered to himself as he went. Neil strained his ear to catch the words, but all he could hear was this, "Ah, dear ones of my own soul!" and this, "O father of my soul, shining in heaven!" When Neil looked forward once more, the vision ahead of him had vanished, and he took up the journey again, pondering this strange thing and finding it beyond belief.

A little later they were climbing up through the wood to the level on which the robbers were set as vultures. Their coming was noticed, for a shaggy man, who had been standing with spear erect at the entrance of their rampart, turned suddenly and disappeared as though to summon those within. Voices, loud and gruff, were heard, one calling and the other answering, and, just as the two men of God reached the gateway, the Nameless One came forward with a company of his villains, all armed with spears or swords, though the chief carried a thick whip, such as they used to control their wolf-hounds. Their brows were dark with rage, and they whispered and nudged one another like men who planned a sudden and treacherous attack.

The blessed man looked more like a king than ever as he halted and cast his calm, stern glance over his enemies. He crossed himself and Neil did likewise. This was the signal for a torrent of the most horrible words to pour from the robber's throat. By the name of the foul monster that lives in Loch na Leárg, and by the name of the naked demons in the black pool of Monamor, he cursed the Saint and God and Christ, and spat as he named the holy names. Molaise felt Neil reel against him, and, turning quickly, bade the lad be of good courage. But it was not fear that moved Neil. At once he recovered, and, leaping forward with a wild cry, would have fallen in fury upon the Nameless One, had not Molaise seized him, bidding him in a loud voice "Keep silence!" The lad obeyed, and stood quivering at the side of the kingly Abbot, while Molaise addressed the robber and said:

"Thou child of Belial, red outlaw from God,

with hands dyed in the blood of holy men and little children, the time of thy miserable end draws on! To-morrow, at break of day, thou shalt be judged of God at the Stone of Judgment on yonder shore. And yet even now confess openly thy great crimes and repent of them, peradventure the compassion of God and men's hearts may be opened to thee!"

On hearing this dread but compassionate word, the robber chief hesitated awhile, but the evil in his heart conquered, and he took a step forward with uplifted whip, then paused, and, turning to his men, ordered them to drive the Abbot away. The villains edged forward to obey, but not very eagerly, for Molaise stood his ground with a bearing so quiet and stern that they turned their heads aside, as dogs do when courage fails them, and drew back in silence. Then Molaise turned on his heel, and, without looking back, walked slowly down the hill, stopping once to pluck a wild rose and set it in his girdle, while Neil, still shaking with great emotion, went quietly with him.

Not till they were well along the meadow towards the shore did Molaise stop and face round to speak to Neil.

"Tell me now, my son," said he, "what hath been revealed to thee!"

"O, my father," cried Neil in reply, "thou knowest!"

"Yea," said the blessed man, "the Nameless One hath a name at last! He is the murderer of thy father and the ravisher of holy Lathglyn far away! Last night I knew it, for it was revealed to me in my soul, when he passed us on the water by the cave. A heavenly voice told me this, when I remembered how four years ago, in the month of July, this man came with three ships to Loch an Eilean and disembarked much precious stuff at Monamor."

"This is all of God," cried Neil, tears running down his cheeks. "O, my lord, could it be that my dead father and the blessed Abbot Artbrannan, who is dead, came hither to us to guide us in this matter?"

Molaise looked quickly at Neil, but said no more in reply than this: "The blessed dead are alive for evermore, my son."

As they moved off again, Neil took courage to ask another question.

"Tell me, good father," said he, "by what power shall the murderous man be brought to judgment to-morrow to the Stone?"

Molaise looked all about him in the sky before answered. "Ah, little Neil," he said at length, "God will provide an escort!"

After this they went in silence along the shore to their little boat, and so crossed to the island.

III

In the late dusk of that day, a boat crept out from Monamor and made a course to the right, keeping close to the dark shore. It held on thus till it reached the point at the open sea, and then made over to the point of Holy Isle. The men who rowed it, and in particular he that held the steering-oar, had no desire to pass within hail of the cave, as they had done on the previous evening. The Nameless One had had enough talk with the Abbot of Holy Isle for one day. They made little enough talk among themselves as they voyaged, and silence had fallen upon them when they reached the great black rocks that rise straight from the water like a quay for ships. Bringing their boat alongside, they made her fast, and, arming themselves with clubs, began to move stealthily along the outer shore of the isle. All was hushed as death, save the eerie lap and leap of the black water against the frowning face of the rocks. An owl hooted from the hill in a long ghostly moan, and the men stopped dead for a moment with a chill at their heart. On again they went, but there was some strange mood and foreboding in the air that night, and the darkness seemed to stare upon them with unwinking eyes. The men kept closer to one another than was their wont, and if one made any noise, however slight, as he crept along, all would stop to make sure that the silence was unbroken otherwise.

Suddenly a voice broke like a bell upon their ears, clear and hollow, from behind a rock twenty paces away! This was the cry of the voice:

"As a beast of the sea is clubbed, so will men club thee, thou monster of the sea!"

The hearts of the robbers seemed turned to stone. They fell prone upon the seaweed, and clutched one another in a terror that made the salt sweat run down their faces upon their parched lips. Again the voice was raised, higher now and wailing above the rock. The robber chief dared to raise himself and look. It was as he had dreaded! In a faint shimmer of the light above the sea-pools, he saw the form of a monk lift itself upon the rock and stand like an image of judgment over him. The robber went blind with fear: his head quaked and shook as though his neck were broken, his throat swelled and choked the cries that struggled in his breast.

"It is the Abbot of Glynn!" he whispered hoarsely. "It is the dead Abbot of Glynn, whom I slew!"

His companions began to make off. Their chief felt them go, and called to them to aid him likewise to escape. But they gave no heed to his crying. It was every man to find his own way in his own strength to get beyond reach of this avenging spectre. So they scuttled away, and, floundering, falling, climbing, leaping, they came to their boat, and, after calling once the name of their chief, they pushed off and rowed away with the strength that terror gives.

Meantime the pirate chief lay in a stupor of fear in the pool beneath the haunted rock. Presently he was aware that the dreaded shape was drawing nearer, but he could move neither hand nor foot. At length he knew that the dead Abbot was bending over him. He heard him say:

"Arise! attend me!"

He could not rise. Sharper came the word of command, and at length the pirate got him to his knees, then slowly to his feet, and stood swaying before the dark ghost.

Suddenly the pirate found tongue and wailed: "O dread servant of God, spare me!" Looking round wildly he cried, "For the sake of thy God and Christ, the child of thy God, save me from thy men-at-arms! They close upon me. Truly I will go with thee: only bid them lower their spears, I beseech thee!"

And thus he wailed, saying these words over and over again. The ghostly monk paused in silence for a while, seeming to look round about him, then, lifting his hand, he beckoned the pirate to follow, and the miserable man obeyed. Up to the shore turf they passed, and along the track by the shore they walked, the one behind the other, and thus they reached the Judgment Stone.

"Lie thou there!" said the dark monk, pointing to the side of the great stone.

"Yea, lord," whined the wretch; "but have thy men-at-arms stand well away from me!"

The other looked all around again, but answered nothing. So the man lay down, and such was the fatigue of his tortured soul, that in a little he was fast asleep. His captor seated himself on the grass beside the Well and waited for dawn to break.

With the first peep of day the watcher by the Judgment Stone heard a sound in the cave above, and, looking up, beheld the Abbot Molaise descending the rough steps that led up to the cell. The watcher arose and awaited his coming.

"Thou here, little Neil?" said Molaise—for, indeed, it was Neil! Then, seeing the shape beside the Judgment Stone, he said quickly, "By the Rood of Oran, what have we here? . . . Ah, he is come then!"

"Yea, lord," answered Neil, "I brought him hither."

"Thou!" cried Molaise.

"Yea, lord," said the lad, and forthwith told his story—how he had stolen off from the monastery at nightfall to the rocks of the seals, how he had won ahead of the pirates as they crept along the shore, how he had lifted up his voice in the dying words of the Abbot Artbrannan, and all that befel thereafter.

Molaise had something like anger in his eyes as he listened, and when the tale was done, he said:

"Did I not say to thee, God will provide an escort? Thou hast done ill in this." And yet the tone of the blessed man's voice grew less stern with every word he uttered. "Well and well, son Neil, did I not say to thee, God will provide an escort? All this livelong night have I spent in prayer that God would beset that evil man with heavenly soldiers who should prick him in his conscience hither. Did I not say to thee, God will provide an escort?"

At this Neil remembered the strange words of the pirate, and told the thing to Molaise. And the Abbot said: "Even so: did I not tell thee?"

Then Molaise said: "Let us awake this sinful man!"

He stooped to him and touched him. But the man slept on. Then he shook him roughly, but still no sign of awaking. Then Molaise knelt beside him, and felt him at his heart and throat and on the thread of life that beats in a man's wrist. Looking up at Neil, he said:

"The man is dead!"

But the Saint remained on his knees and prayed awhile.

THE VIKINGS: THE GUIDE

THE VIKINGS: THE GUIDE

"*They had no cause to boast that they in war's work*
The better men were in the battle stead,
At the conflict of banners, at the meeting of spears,
At the concourse of men, at the traffic of weapons."

—Battle of Brunanburh.

IT would be difficult to find a single boy, or even a single girl who does not love to hear stories about the Vikings. You have a fine picture inside your head of the tall warriors with the fair hair, and the glittering helmets with the ox-horns or feathery wings curved above them; their scarlet cloaks hanging over their backs and caught at the throat by a great gold brooch; their burly legs wrapped in cloth and laced around and across with thongs; their round shields painted gold, black, blue, yellow; their giant swords and battle-axes, and their clubs of wood studded with mighty nails. And in the picture in your mind you see the long ships in which they sailed to war, with the wooden image of a dragon or bristling serpent lifting itself high above the bow; the great square sail with a raven sometimes drawn upon it, and the gunwale plated with the rows of the warriors' shields.

Wonderfully brave and daring were these old men of the *viks!* That is the meaning of the word Viking—*vik-men*. We are apt to think that the word means some kind of "king." Well, no: they were the men of the *vik,* that is a "creek," the word we find in Wick in Caithness or in Brodick which means the "broad bay." Wonderfully brave and daring those old warriors were; but they were cruel, without pity, and they destroyed so much that was good and beautiful and holy in the west of Scotland that we are not quite sure whether they are altogether the romantic heroes which the coloured illustrations in children's story-books make them out to be.

The Vikings came to Arran. Not only so, but they settled in Arran. Indeed, for more than 300 years the Vikings were the rulers of Arran. They have left traces of themselves all about the island, in graves and forts and names cut in the face of rocks and in names which they gave to bays and hills and farms.

Now, when did they come to Arran? They began to come about the year A.D. 800. At first only odd ships came. The Vikings set out from Norway and captured the Orkney and Shetland Islands to begin with, then they made raids on the mainland and the islands right round the north and west of Scotland, landing from their ships, slaying, robbing, burning, and so many came and so often, that they conquered at last all those coasts and the east coast of Ireland as well, and the Isle of Man. It was as they were winning their way south by the Mull of Kintyre, that odd ships came raiding up the Firth of Clyde to give the old Gaelic clans of Arran their first battle with the Norse Ravens.

Fifty years later or so, in A.D. 870, a great Viking fleet sailed up past Ailsa Craig and Pladda, and anchored in Lamlash Bay. It was commanded by a Danish Viking named Ivar the Boneless, and a Norse Viking, Olaf the White, who was called King of Dublin. Three years before, Ivar had been away in England, leading his victorious Vikings as far as York. Now he was on his way with Olaf and his men to Alcluyd, which we call Dumbarton, the capital of the Britons and their kingdom of Strathclyde. And they put in at Lamlash Bay on their voyage, in order to trim their ships and pull themselves together, before going north to the attack. It took them four months to capture Alcluyd.

It was about this time that the Vikings gained possession of Arran. But do not think that they did this all at once. In bays like Brodick, on sandy shores like Sannox, up the mouth of burns like Monamor in Lamlash and Achancairn and Ashdale in Whiting Bay, at little coves like the one inside King's Cross Point, they drove their ships ashore, and, leaping out, made with sword and axe and spear against the Gaelic villages, as a rule successfully, but sometimes in vain, for brave men are at their bravest in defending their homes: so that presently the Vikings were settled at many points round the island coast. Those whom the Vikings captured would become slaves to them; but others would take refuge in the high glens and hold out there, though their life must have been hard and miserable. Then gradually the two races would mingle, as indeed happened, and the inhabitants of the island become partly Norse and partly Celtic in blood, with the Gaelic tongue as much in use among them as the speech of the Norse. Such mixed people in the west Highlands and Islands were called the Gall-Gaels, that is, the Stranger Gaels.

When the King of Norway was at the height of his power, he ruled Norway and islands and mainland in the north and down the west of Scotland, and south to the Isle of Man. This was a very scattered kingdom to keep in order, and, as time went on, various chiefs along that long line showed a desire for independence. This happened in the north, where the Earl of Orkney acted like a king on his own, and in the south, where the lord of Man called himself a king. Half-way between these two, that is in Argyll, a great Gaelic or Dalriadic chief called Somerled began, afterwards, to cock his bonnet! All this annoyed the King of Norway, and several times he came with a great fleet to bring such proud princes to their senses. Thus King Magnus came from Norway in 1090 and 1098, striking terror everywhere by the cruelty of his punishments. He sailed to Arran on those occasions, and once again great Viking fleets anchored in the loch of Lamlash.

But now a new power began to endanger the might of Norway in the west of Scotland. This was the kingdom which at first was called Alba and then Scotia. It included all the mainland of Scotland, and the king was called the King of Scots. These Scottish kings, when they had made one kingdom of the mainland, began to turn their eyes to the Norse possessions in the west. Hakon, King of Norway, became alarmed, and sent a great fleet under Ospak in 1230 to strengthen his position against the Scots. Ospak sailed with his ships down the west and up the Firth of Clyde to Lamlash, and then on to Rothesay, where he captured the castle after a hard fight which lasted three days. Then Ospak died of sickness. Alexander II., the Scottish king, planned a blow in return against Norway, and, mustering a fleet in 1249, sailed away round the Mull of Kintyre, and got as far as Oban, where he died. His son, Alexander III. of Scots, took up the quarrel, but now King Hakon was thoroughly roused. In 1263 he took to sea with a powerful fleet. He was joined by Magnus of Man and the Somerled chiefs and all the chiefs in the west except Ewen of Argyll. Round the Mull sailed Hakon, and by the usual sea-track of the Vikings up the Firth to the anchorage in the shelter of Eilean Molaise or Melansay, as the Vikings called the Holy Isle. Proudly the long dragon-prows foamed their way through the narrow strait at King's Cross, the great striped square-sails bellying forward, the banners, pictured with black ravens, fluttering at the mast-head, the shields along the vessels' sides shining like great flat beads in their bright paint, the shaggy rowers pulling, with long easy strokes, down the wind, the yellow oars moving to and fro like the legs of some dread sea-slug. The king's ship was leading, a great vessel with a dragon's head forward, plated with shimmering gold, and its thirty-seven benches for rowers. Swinging round in the open waters of the loch, they swept forward to their stations, and, as the sails were slacked away and came crumpling down the mast, oars were backed, and the souse of the great anchors hissed from ship to ship. The king looked round upon his vessels riding up to their moorings, saw the rowers bump the long oars on the gunwale and heave them upright in the air, as one man, before they shipped them, heard the deep voices of his men flinging about the jests which men make when a voyage is over, and he paced his poop with pride lighting up his face, and a word of coarse contempt on his tongue for the upstart King of Scots.

In a few weeks Hakon was back again in Lamlash Bay, but now the wings of the Ravens were sadly clipped. That happened at Largs. At Largs it was on Wednesday, October 3, 1263, that a great storm burst on his fleet, and the knights and spearmen of Alexander, the Scottish king, fell on his warriors, and the proud King of Norway gathered his battered forces away and put back to Lamlash. He told his men he would pass the winter in Ireland, and bring war up the Clyde again in spring. But his men would not agree. So away northward through the Hebrides sailed the stricken king, stricken by defeat and fatally stricken in health, for when he reached Kirkwall in Orkney, he was carried ashore and there he died. His death marks the end of the Norse dominion in Scotland. For a sum of money (never paid) his successor sold his Scottish realm to the King of Scots, all save Orkney and Shetland, which for sometime longer called the King of Norway their over-lord.

Ah, well, the Vikings have all vanished away and long ago! To-day, as we walk pleasantly about the shores of Arran, or move across its bays in little boats, with pretty names like "Heather Bell" or "Violet," it is difficult to believe that over these shingle banks the fierce warriors waded from their ships to the shore, with murderous weapons in their hands and the fury of slaughter in their eyes. Little children with their brown legs trail chubby little yachts by a string through the warm shallows on the sand, where once the great boots of the sea-rovers splashed their way to the beach; and round the rocky headlands boys trawl for mackerel where once the dragon-ships crawled along, looking for an opening to strike in their sharp beaks. If the surface of the sea could keep the marks that keels make, as a soft road keeps the mark of wheels, we should see all these blue waters about Arran scored and furrowed in every direction with the tracks of the ships, as closely as the threads of a fishing-net. But the waves have blotted them out for ever. When I was a little lad and stood on these hills, wondering at the long lanes of calm water which one sometimes sees glistening in the Firth, when everywhere else the dark blue water is rippled by the breeze, I was told that the long passages of calm water were the tracks of ghost-ships of the old sea-kings! Then I would gaze long and hard with round eyes, in the hope that I might catch a glimpse of the ships themselves; misty forms they would be, white and transparent as ghosts are said to be. But I never saw the phantoms that were sailing there, although sometimes I almost made myself believe I did. No: they have vanished away and long ago! So distant it all seems to-day, that for many people their very name is like a name "writ in water."

But stay! I can show you their name written on something harder than water. You have learnt how often the ships of the Vikings came to anchor in the shelter of Holy Isle. You may guess how pleased the mariners were to reach that quiet haven. As is the way of men after a voyage, did they not say to one another, "Let's go ashore and stretch our legs a bit!" Or the fresh water had run low in the ship, and so, lowering the ship's boat over the side, they bumped the empty water-kegs aboard, which sounded like drums as they struck the thwarts, and the men followed after, with their stiff sea-legs, and so pulled to the beach. Along the shore track afterwards they would wander, sniffing the scent of thyme and wild garlic, and having horse-play with one another as they went. Then the cave [25] of the vanished Saint would catch their eye, and up they would go, inquisitive as boys. And here and there a man who had the wonderful gift of writing letters would draw his knife, and with its sharp point begin, as boys will, to carve his name inside the cave on the face of the rock, in long thin letters which stand up and cross one another at the top like stalks of grass, tall and withered. That is in very truth what they did, for the letters are there to this day, some of them worn away, but still clear enough to enable skilful scholars to read them. Some years ago a drawing of them was sent to such scholars in Sweden, and again (in July, 1911) two such scholars came to Holy Isle, called Magnus Olsen and Hakon Schetelig (a real Viking sound about these names, isn't there?), and thus they read the names:—"Nikulos of Haene cut" is the first, and the others are "Sveinn" and "Quondr cut the runes" and "Amundr" and "Olafr" and "Joan" (John) and the letter "M," and lastly "Vigleikr the stallari cut." The word "stallari" means a Marshall. Vigleikr, we know, was Marshall to King Hakon; and, as Dr. Magnus Olsen says, "In all probability Vigleikr cut the inscription in September, 1263, when the Norwegian fleet was in Lamlash Bay." The others may belong to the same time, but the one which reads "Olafr" is two hundred years older.

But there are other traces of the Viking period besides the runes in the Cave of St. Molaise in Holy Isle. To the time of the Vikings belong the round forts which can still be seen in Arran. These are to begin with Gaelic forts, but doubtless the Norse both used and maintained them.

Let me tell you where the forts are to be found. There is a splendid one on a height on the north side of North Glen Sannox. It is called *Torr an t-Sean Chaisteil,*[1] which means "Hill of the Old Fort." The fort is made of two round ramparts, the second being three-quarters of a circle and attached to the other as an outer defence on its west side. The entrance is on the east side, and was guarded by two walls which came around it like two tusks. Of these two walls like tusks only those stones remain which formed its gateway. Thus the fort had two gateways, but, as you enter the first gateway, you find that the inner gateway is not straight in front of you but off to the right. This was done so that if an attack got in at the first gateway, it had to swerve before reaching the second. Right opposite the inner gateway, across the circle, you see the remains of a small cell or hut-dwelling within the wall: there are traces of other two hut-dwellings. The walls of the fort were originally about twelve feet high.

Another fort is at *Glencloy.*[17] It is sometimes called "The Fairy's Mound," but the name in Gaelic does not mean that, but "The Hill of the Old Fort," exactly like the one in North Glen Sannox. Another name it gets is "Bruce's Castle," but while it is altogether likely that King Robert the Bruce came here, it was not he that made it. This fort has not been dug up, and so there is nothing to be seen except a green mound. A traveller in 1772 wrote about it and said that "a great dike" was here, surrounding a fort; probably the stones of it were taken away to build dykes for the fields.

Another fort is *Dun Fionn*[18] at Lamlash, at a height of 450 feet on the hill which runs down to Clachlands point. Some have connected this spot with Finn or Fingal, but the name really means "The Fair Fort." All that is to be seen now is part of a low mound enclosing a space some 40 yards long by 16 yards wide.

Another fort is at *Glen Ashdale,*[32] a little way down the stream from the waterfall, on the high ground (550 feet above sea-level) to the right of the fall as you go up the glen. It is in the wood. The wall of the fort is visible, 5 feet high in places, but it must have been a very high wall, as it measures 15 feet in thickness on the ground.

Another fort is at *King's Cross*[30] on the little height above the Point. The circle enclosed by the wall is about 35 feet across. The wall itself was made by building up two parallel walls of great stones and filling these in with small stones and earth. It is on an average 12 feet thick. The stones are red sandstone, and were probably brought by the builders from Holy Isle.

Close to this fort at King's Cross, 23 feet to the south of it, you see a shallow digging on the surface, boat-like in shape, about 30 feet long. This is a most interesting find.[29] In 1909, when the green mound which covered it was removed, it was found to have been a Viking's grave. A slab of bone, with ring carving on it, rivets of a ship, nails, and a bronze coin, were discovered. These all bore signs of having been burnt. The coin is called a "styca," minted by Wigmund, an Archbishop of York (his name is on it), whose dates are A.D. 837-854. From these facts the picture of what happened at this grave long ago is fairly clear and plain. This is the grave of one of the warrior chiefs who followed Ivar the Boneless in his raids in England, and then sailed with him and Olaf of Dublin to the siege of Alcluyd in A.D. 870. How the chief died we know not, but here at King's Cross they pulled a ship's boat from the water, and setting it on this little headland, placed the dead Viking upon it, and gave him his funeral of fire. When the flames expired, they raked together the ashes of the dead and the scorched rivets of the ship and its nails and the little coin, and then built the high mound of earth and stones over all.

Another Viking's grave was discovered in 1896 at Lamlash, near the south bank of Blairmore Burn, when a mound was being removed to build a house there. The boss or great central knob of a Viking's shield was found, and also fragments of his sword.

Thus you see that in unexpected ways and places we still can behold marks of the old sea-rovers from Norway who invaded Arran and held it for so many years. I said that traces of them still remain in the names of glens and bays and hills and farms in Arran. Perhaps you would like to hear some of these, so I give you the following list, working southward from Sannox: *Sannox,* Sand vik, sandy bay; *Merkland,* mark land (rental sum); *Brodick,* Breidavik, broad bay; *Goatfell,* Geita-fell, goat mountain; *Ormidale,* Orm's dale; *Rosa,* Hross-à, horse river; *String Road,* strengr, a cord; *Corriegills,* Korfa-gil, ravens' gully; *Benlister,* Penny-land of Alister (rental sum); *Whiting Bay,* huit thing, white place of Assembly (but this is very doubtful: the Bay is probably named after the whiting fish); *Kiscadale,* Kistudalr, coffin-dale; *Glenashdale,* Askr-dale, ash-dale; *Dippin,* Tvi-penninga, two-penny land (rental sum); *Pladda,* Flat-ey, flat island.

THE VIKINGS: THE STORY

THE VIKINGS: THE STORY

"The Tale of Sigurd and Angus"

I

YOU have walked, have you not, from Whiting Bay to King's Cross Point, and you know how the track leaves the shore and slants upwards through the hazels and then on to the Doons at the Point. As you walk along that hill-side above the shore, you have seen at a little distance on your left a row of houses with old trees sheltering them, and a flagstaff standing up like a tall spear. This clachan is called Woodhill, and it is there that my story begins.

What I am going to tell you did not happen yesterday or the day before, but a thousand years ago, in the year 870. The houses of Woodhill were not there, of course, but other cottages were there, not altogether unlike the ones you see to-day, but not so cosy-looking or so well built, and not so sweetly white-washed, and not so pleasantly planted with roses and fuschias about the doors. No, it was a dreary cluster of gray houses that stood there then, built unevenly of rough stones and thatched thickly with rushes and heather that had become black and green with smoke and age. They looked even drearier than that, because more than half of the houses had been destroyed by fire, and the grey walls looked like stone-coffins with the charred timbers of the roof pointing to the sky, like the rib bones of a great beast's skeleton. There were no hedges then. Little fields had been made by clearing back the growth of hazels and brambles, and in these corn struggled for life in the stony yellow earth, much shorter and thinner than the corn we grow. Against the gables of the houses brown piles of peat were stacked, and rude fishing-nets were stretched to dry between poles of silver birch, set up before the huts.

From the roof of several of the houses a trickle of smoke floats up into the still October evening. It helps to cheer us a little to see that smoke, for everything else, and all around, looks as sad and mournful as can be. There will be frost to-night: already the cold begins to chill our necks and backs. Even the burning red of the sky in the west has a lonely and unfriendly look. It is an evening for good company (it is indeed) and a jolly meal and a big fire, with song and story in the cheerful blaze of it, while outside the moon will rise like a vast lantern in the mist, and the grass stiffen with rime, and the wet places of the tracks take on their crust.

It will be difficult, I fear, to find such a company in this uncanny and dreary clachan. And yet there is a good fire surely in that biggest of the cottages over there, and don't you hear the sound of voices that may be making merry, for they are certainly loud enough. Let us draw near with good heart then, and knock at the low door, for, although this all happens a thousand years ago, Gaelic hospitality was as kindly then as it has ever been.

We find ourselves within a rough dwelling indeed. In the centre of the floor a fire of peat burns, while the smoke goes up through a hole in the thatch—most of it, that is, for much of it floats about the darkness up there and on the level of the inmates, making it difficult to make anything of them out at first, except their faces, which the fire-light illumines. There is a smell of cattle, and well there may be, because the byre is along there to the left, with no wall between it and this dwelling-room, and you can hear the little cows moving in the straw and the sound of their munching. Above the cows, on cross-benches, fowls must be roosting; you can hear their lazy croak from time to time.

But let us take note of the people among whom we find ourselves. There are nine men among them, and these are seated around the fire.

Several youths stand behind them, while in corners to the right women gather together, some with babes in their arms, others white with age, and one old crone who sits apart, bent like a witch upon a stick, and muttering to herself. You will look tenderly upon this old witch when I tell you that four months ago she lost in death her husband and her three sons and the seven children of these three sons. How did they die? They died under the red swords of the Vikings. Four months ago a great fleet of those fierce sea-rovers rounded the Point from the south, and poured into Loch an Eilean, which is Lamlash Bay. So suddenly they came that the Gaels of such villages as this had barely time to get their women and children away, and a few of their cattle, to the high glen of Achancairn, when two dragon-ships emptied their fierce crews in the little bay at the Point, and, like a wind of death, the Vikings swept over the village, killing all that met them, tossing the goods of the houses out of doors, and setting the roofs ablaze. The villagers were outnumbered and taken by surprise, and, although many of them did brave deeds and laid many a Norseman low, they were driven back at last and away. Next day the dread ships gathered themselves together and sailed northward under their admirals, Ivar the Boneless and Olaf the White, to harry Bute and to strike a deadly blow against Alcluyd, which is now Dumbarton.

It is of these things the men around the fire are talking now. They are holding a council, and these are the chief men of this clachan and the clachan at Achancairn and the clachan at Cnocan-choilich.

"More and more they will be coming, often and oftener still!" an old man is saying, and the others nod their heads sadly, as over a thing that is bound to be. "It is the better thing to gather away to the head of Achancairn and there be making ready."

"Never now!" replies a young man, the tallest and comeliest of them all. This is Angus Mac Cuaig, the head of this broken village. "Never now, Ean Dhu!" he says again, addressing the old man. "Will you have the sons of Erc and the children of Molaise of blessed memory to leave these sacred shores like goats that scatter when a dog barks on the hill? Will you have the ghost of my dead father come across from Eilean Molaise and find this hearth-stone cold and black? By the Stone of Judgment and the blood of my brother and my sweet mother, I will fight them where I be, let who will flee to the far hollows of Achancairn!"

"Be you gentle, Angus Mac Cuaig," replies Ean Dhu; "it is but for a little while we gather there.

For see and hear again what Fergus tells us. Alcluyd of the Britons has fallen and the fleet of the pirates comes south again. Tell it again, Fergus!"

"The tale hath a beard by now," interrupts Angus, rising and looking angrily round the circle. "Mary, woman," says he, turning round, "put a pot on the peat, and let the women come to the fire!"

This was a bitter thing to say: it meant that he thought little of the men. And the men felt this. So they rose up with dark looks and in a mind to break off the council. But Ean Dhu laid his hands on their arms and besought Angus to be gentle, when the old witch got up slowly, and, hobbling on her stick, pushed her way to the fire and lifted up her shrill voice against Angus.

"Peace, old hag!" cried the young chief.

"Peace!" repeated the woman, pointing a skinny finger. "You are fey, Angus Mac Cuaig, fey, fey, fey!" and, as she said this, her voice hushed, and she seemed to be looking far away, seeing far things. "Aye, green the grass by the Dùn, but eh, the red blood and the white foam upon his lips! And the raven and the dove both lie dead!" She swayed as she spoke, and the tall men stooped to her and led her to a bench, and there she sat and drew her hand across her eyes, while low moans sounded from her old white lips.

Silence fell on them all, broken suddenly and fearfully by a knock at the door. Angus was the first to recover himself, and, striding forward, flung open the door. Against the moonlight stood a muffled figure, in a long robe, caught at the waist by a rope, a cowl over his head, and a tall staff in his hand.

"Come you in, father! It is the holy Abbot Colmain," said Angus; and the Abbot entered, shambling in his walk, but blessing the house and all therein in the name of Christ and Molaise and Michael.

The others hastened to make room for him, and, gathering again around the fire, saw how pale he was and how hollow his cheeks were, and a strange glitter in his eyes. They wondered if the yellow Norsemen were already in the Loch, that the Abbot had left Eilean Molaise and the ruins of the monastery and come to them. Nay, it was not so, they learned when they questioned him. The Abbot was alone on the holy island, but could no longer bear to be alone, and so he had come over to them.

"Ochone, my children," he said to them, "dear to me was the Family in Eilean Molaise, and they are all gone away, and I alone abide, with the little ones of my soul all dead. I cannot lose from my throat the smell of the burning, and from my eyes the sight of their red blood. And I buried them all, not one was left for the birds; I buried them all when the wild men had sailed away in their serpent ships. But woe is me for the monastery of the blessed man Molaise! How can I build it with tears, and tears are all that I have: and how can I create monks with prayers, and prayers are all I can give?"

Thus speaking, the Abbot bowed his head and wept, and the women wailed softly, and the men too wept, but silently. That had been the crowning woe of the Vikings' raid, when the whole monastery on the Holy Isle had been given to the flames and the monks all slain except Colmain.

" Come now, good father," said Angus, " we will be building the holy place most surely again. Lift up your heart! Maybe the pirates will come no more, and we will get young lads to be monks for you, and the bells will be heard across the loch as ever before."

" Angus, my dear son," said Colmain, " this is the end of the world!"

Anger burned in the young chief's eyes, but he did not reply. The others told the Abbot how they had a mind to retreat to the hills, since the ships of the foe were coming south again, and the Abbot said: " In a vision of the night I have seen the green shores of Arran black with ravens, and they snapped their red beaks over the dead. This is the end of the world!"

Then they said to one another: "Sorrow and loneliness have chilled the holy man; may Christ and Columcille and Lais heal his broken heart. Come, Angus, if this be the end of the world, we will stand by you! But send you the women and the bairns, as we will, to yon safe hollow up Achancairn."

At this Angus took them by the hands and said loudly, "Sons of Erc, hail!" And, rising up, he drew his sword, and cried: "Arran of the Gael, land of heroes, mother of saints, hail!" And, as torch lights torch, his heart set fire to theirs, and they too leapt up and cried, "Arran of the Gael!"

The Abbot hardly seemed to notice. He had taken from beneath his cloak a book with little pictures in gold and blue and green round the edges of the fine black writing, and he was looking at its last unfinished page and saying, "Here his pen slipped, when they broke on us through the mist. Here it slipped, the pen of my son Libran: it looks like the slash of a sword!" And the old crone was sitting bent upon her stick, and muttering to herself words about a raven and a dove and a red dye on the green grass by the Dùn.

II

Next morning a wind from the north was blowing down the Firth of Clyde, and the white horses of the waves were foaming across the blue field of the sea. Between the islands of Bute and Cumbrae the fleet of Ivar the Boneless and Olaf the White was streaming southward, with their sails so full of wind that the rowers had shipped their oars and were taking their ease in the sunny hollow of their ships. Some were asleep, exhausted by the long siege of Alcluyd and the riotous behaviour that followed its capture; others were playing bones upon the rowers' benches, gambling their plunder; and the wounded men lay beside them, white and weary, but with thankful hearts that they were out on the good sea again.

At the tail of the fleet sailed two ships called the *Wolf* and the *Long Bear.* The captain of these was Sigurd the Blue Pine, so-called from his great lithe height and the colour of his arms and cloak. He lay on a pile of bear-skins on the poop of the *Wolf,* and beside him sat his foster-brother, Svein the Seal, a man whom no shipwreck could drown. Below them, where the poop drops to the well with its benches for the oars, sat Gundr the scald, which means a bard or minstrel, and Gundr pressed a harp against his breast with his left hand, which was bandaged by reason of a wound, and with his right he stroked the strings and made strange music to the song he sang. He was singing the deeds of Sigurd which he did at Alcluyd, how he it was that climbed the high rock with the crews of the *Wolf* and the *Long Bear* and captured the topmost fort, which none of the men of Ivar and Olaf could take. And Gundr, as he sang, made verses which spoke bitterly of Ivar and Olaf, and accused them of jealousy against Sigurd and of robbing him of the glory due him and the spoil he should have got. But these verses Gundr sang less loudly, lest other ships might hear. The crew of the *Wolf* heard well enough, and they growled in approval of the song, and Sigurd's brow grew dark and his hand gripped his dagger as he looked forward at the banners of the admirals dancing in the sunshine at the head of the tossing line of the fleet.

Gundr finished his song, and Sigurd filled the cup that lay beside him on the deck and handed it to the scald to drink. This was a golden cup which Sigurd had taken from the altar of a little church in Bute, where with his own hand he had slain the priest. Then, turning to Svein, his foster-brother, said Sigurd:

"I grow weary of following this Olaf as a sheep follows the shepherd to be shorn. I grow weary of following this jelly-fish Ivar to have him pick my bones. And you know that I cannot return to the Dùn of Dublin and the why of that! And you know that I cannot return to Norroway and the why of that as well!"

Svein knew the why and the wherefore of these things. Sigurd was marked for death by bitter enemies to whom he had done vile things there.

"What then to do, and where to go, Svein, my brother?" he said after a pause.

Svein answered nothing, for he knew that his lord had some plan brewing. And so it was, for again Sigurd spake and said:

"There is a little bay in Hersey, a green bay and good fields near Melansay (it was thus the Vikings called Arran and Holy Isle), a green bay and good fields, where we fared very well four months ago, brother Svein! Not all the houses were burned, and the corn will be gathered now, and it is a good hillside for hunting. What say you to plant the clan of the Blue Pine and to breed your Seals in the land above that green bay, Svein, my brother?"

Svein was very glad to fall in with the scheme of his chief, for he, too, had few doors open to him in the lands to which the rovers were returning. He went down among the men and spoke to them of Sigurd's plan, and found all willing.

The two now hoped that the leaders of the fleet would choose to sail right past Arran and the loch behind Holy Isle. That was likely, for such a wind as was driving them along would carry them quick and sure to Ireland, whither they desired to come. As they swept across the wide sea between Garroch Head in Bute and the mountainous shore of Arran, it was clear that Ivar and Olaf intended to neglect the harbour of Lamlash. Their heads bore off several points to the east of Holy Isle. The summit of Goatfell was still smoking with the morning mist, but real smoke was going up in volumes from point to point upon the lower hills. On Dùn Fionn in particular a great column of warning smoke arose. These were the beacons of the Gaels, signalling from headland to headland along the coast the approach of the Ravens. But that day the dreaded ships sailed past and away, all but two, the ships of Sigurd the Blue Pine, the *Wolf* and the *Long Bear*.

As the main fleet came over against Holy Isle, plunging along among the white waves, Sigurd gave orders to his men to slack away the sheets of the great sails. The foot of the sails flapped forward and the wind was spilled, so that more and more the ships lagged behind the others. Slowly the tiller was put over to port and the vessels drew off to the right and headed for the northern entrance of Lamlash Bay. The ships ahead gave no sign that they saw the movement, and presently the hill of Holy Isle came between them and the deserters. In past the rock that lies like a whale off Clachlands Point snored the *Wolf* and the *Long Bear,* and within the shelter of the loch they sailed smoothly now but fast. Round to the left they swept, past the ruins of the monastery, and there ahead of them, at King's Cross, they saw the little green bay and the good fields which were the desire of Sigurd's weary but greedy heart.

From stem to stern of the vessels all was got ready for the landing. Men strapped around them their leather tunics plated with metal, swords were girded about their waists, spears were laid ready to their hands, the shields were loosened from the gunwale and buckled on brawny arms. Sigurd and the chief warriors made forward to the bow to be ready for the leap when the ships took the ground, and thus they bore down upon the little bay.

III

What Fergus had reported about the return of the Vikings was true. Early that morning Angus Mac Cuaig saw the warning smoke go up on Dùn Fionn. He blew a battle-call on his horn, and its wild notes went echoing to Achancairn. Very speedily the little clans of Angus and Ean and Fergus of Cnocan-choilich had gathered to the

Point. They stood in groups on the sward beneath the round dùn, in which they would assemble themselves should the enemy land in force. Fine braw men they looked, with their long dark-blue plaids twisted about their loins, so that it formed a kilt below and then carried round the broad chest and over the left shoulder, so as to leave the sword-arm free. Their spears stood stacked in bristling bunches. Their naked swords shone in the sun. Upon a great flat rock some had placed their bows and quivers, and were busy setting bowstring and arrows right. From time to time all threw keen glances at a point on the ridge of Mullach Mor of Holy Isle across the strait, for there Angus had two men posted who should watch for the sails of the Ravens flying from the north.

At last the signal came. A long plaintive cry came down the wind across the water, and they looked and saw the sentinels on Mullach Mor wave a white cloth above their heads and then come hastening down the hill to their boat. With slow steps but with alert brave faces, the Gaels moved towards the dùn and took up their places within it. Already the entrance had been filled up with great stones and earth, and capped with whins pulled tightly between the stones. The archers made their way with a few spearmen down to the rocks that flank the little bay on either side, and there they took up their stations, out of sight of anyone coming from the sea.

Then followed that hardest time, the time of waiting before the enemy is seen face to face. Angus moved about, outside the rampart, slapping his thigh and making jests to those within, which made the younger men laugh indeed, but a little uneasily.

Suddenly all talk and laughter were hushed. Out at sea, beyond Holy Isle, there shot into sight the foaming long-ships of the foe! Out at sea! and holding straight away! Could it be true? Were the Ravens flying past them in peace? It seemed too good to be true. They waited to see, minute by minute, hushed and hardly breathing. Then up went hands in joy and a great cry of gladness rose from the fort: the shining ships were scudding straight along! Presently they were off Largie Mor, off Largie Beg, and now the vanguard of the fleet had rounded the utmost headland out of sight!

But the joy was short-lived. An archer at the rocks in the bay called with another note in his voice. All turned towards him, and there in the loch they beheld two ships steering past the ruined *cashel* of the monks, and bearing down fast upon the little bay. So speedily they came that the Gaels had hardly time to recover their discipline when the dragon-ships sludged aground in the shallows of the bay, the sails floated free, a shouting rose, and the first of the tall Vikings leapt into the sea and came splashing towards the shore. Bows twanged behind the rocks and the arrows flew. Three of the yellow-haired invaders reeled and fell in the waves, their red cloaks rising like balloons above them as they lay. But the others made forward without a pause. Again and again the arrows sped, but mostly in vain. Quickly the archers gathered themselves together and retreated, wheeling about from time to time to wing another flight of arrows, and so at last got them to the dùn, and clambered over the ramparts.

And now the Vikings assembled themselves in order and came on with determined faces to assault the fort. The numbers on both sides were about equal, and the Vikings saw that this was a battle worthy of their steel. Crying aloud the names of Sigurd and Thor, they rushed forward and up, some straight ahead, others to the right and around to take the Gaels on the other side. And now the fight surges fiercely. Here a Viking leaps on the wall with axe lifted high to strike, and is smitten back, writhing in his blood. There a Gael, breaking his sword on the glittering helmet of a foe, seizes a huge stone from the wall in both hands, and plunges the mass of it among the sweating, cursing climbers below. A spear, flung as straight and strong as the dive of a gannet takes him in the face, and with arms flung wide he falls dead within the dùn. Thus the battle sways to and fro. But the Gaels are holding their own, and the Norsemen show signs of tiring. Then Svein the Seal gives forth his battle-cry, and, calling to the men, bursts forward on the wall, climbing like a madman, and leaps within! Here is danger indeed: but his followers fail to follow and he is inside alone. Angus Mac Cuaig springs forward to engage him. Brightly flashes his sword, swiftly it falls, and through the plated breast of Svein it goes and the Viking grunts horribly and falls dead. Taking him by the neck of his breast-plate, Angus drags him up the wall and casts the body down. At the feet of Sigurd his foster-brother it falls and lies.

After this the Vikings fell back, pulling away and carrying off some of their wounded men. They gathered themselves together half a bow-shot from the dùn, and there they waited till the chiefs should take counsel together as to the next move in the mournful game. Sigurd stood among them, quivering with rage and grief. His eyes were fixed on the body of Svein lying yonder beneath the wall. His friends spoke to him, but got no answer. Without a word he broke away from them, and, walking slowly, moved straight across to where his dead brother lay. Silence came down on all, and they waited to see what would happen, both Norse

"Rushing like stags in deadly crash."—P. 125.

and Gael. Sigurd stooped over the body and stroked the white face, then rising up he pointed at Angus above him on the wall, and made signs which all understood. He challenged Angus Mac Cuaig to single combat. Angus signalled that he agreed, and all lifted their voices in a shout of approval. Then Sigurd went back to his people to get his arms again, and the Gaels saw him make it plain to them that they should keep their distance, and the Gaels, as courteous warriors, lined the wall of the dùn but went no further. So Angus and Sigurd came forth and faced each other on the green sward between them, as on a field of play.

They fought with swords and shields, at first warily, for each knew the mettle of the other. But soon their blood warmed to the blows, and the swords rang and ground upon each other, and the round shields sounded like drums beneath the valiant strokes, and the tall heroes reeled and recovered, circling round, rushing like stags in deadly crash, pausing and breathing loud.

Angus was first to draw blood. A great red stain appeared on the left side of Sigurd's head beneath his helmet, and spread down his cheek and neck. But a blow fell from his sword, and the shield of Angus burst in twain. This was the beginning of the end. Sigurd took Angus with a great slash across his flank, and before the blow was done, the Gael drove his sword between the other's thighs. Both sank to their knees, but even so the fight went on. Even so the red swords rose and fell mightily still, and then each dealt the last grim stroke that brings death. Their spirits fled away and their bodies fell huddled together on the darkened grass.

A hush fell on the watching ranks. In little groups they came forward to the dead. The desire of further battle was extinguished. The Gaels lifted the body of Angus upon their shields and bore him away to the village. The Norsemen carried dead Sigurd to the knoll beside the dùn, and there they made ready the place of his burial. From the *Long Bear* they dragged the ship's-boat, and resin too they carried. From the woods they brought the withered whins, and dry driftwood from the shore. And they laid the boat in the hollow they had scraped on the knoll, and the dead Sigurd upon the boat with his sword and shield, and a thrall of the dead chief cast his own purse upon the pile. Then Gundr the scald struck a spark from flint and steel and the pile was set afire. Thus Sigurd went home. When the fire had died, they gathered all together, and made the cairn of stones above the hot ashes of the boat and the blackened bones. The stones they took from the rampart of the dùn. Before evening had come, the Vikings had out their ships in the deep water, and at morn they spread the sail and sailed away.

That evening the men of Arran ferried over the body of Angus Mac Cuaig to the Holy Isle, and the bodies of them that likewise were slain in the battle. Six boats rowed across to the sacred place of graves beside the ruined monastery. And the Abbot Colmain sang the sweet words of Christian hope as they laid them in their quiet graves. But the old witch would keep breaking in on the man of God with eerie words. "Achanie," she wailed, "the raven and the dove both lie dead."

THE BRUCE: THE GUIDE

THE BRUCE: THE GUIDE

Into that time the noble king
With his fleet and a few menye,
Three hundred I trow they might well be,
Was to the sea furth of Arane.

—BARBOUR'S *Brus.*

THERE is one date in history which no good Scots bairn ever forgets, and that is the year 1314. What happened then? Bannockburn, of course! On June 24, 1314, the Scots who had bled with Wallace and had rallied to the leadership of King Robert the Bruce, laid the power of proud Edward low, and brought liberty to auld Scotland.

But what has Arran got to do with Bruce and Bannockburn? A great deal, as you shall presently hear. I don't know whether any company of the men of Arran fought at the great battle. Some people say they did, other people say they didn't. Those who say that they did remind us that a band of heroic soldiers called "the Brandanes" fought at Bannockburn, and under Wallace as well at the fatal field of Falkirk, and they declare that the Brandanes meant men of Bute and Arran. But other people say "No:

the name of the Brandanes did indeed come to include the men of Arran, but that was long after the time of Bannockburn; at the time of Bannockburn the name meant only the men of Bute."

We shall leave this quarrel alone, I think; it will probably never be quite settled. But even if we have to give up the belief that there was a company of Arran men at Bannockburn, in the battalion of the Brandanes, we do know that Bruce did have brave men from our island under his banner. We know quite surely of two, and it would be strange if there were not more, because the great King came through Arran on the way to win his crown, and stayed here some time, and he had a wonderful way of gaining the loyalty and service of men, especially those who were oppressed by tyrants, as the people of Arran were at that time.

As I have just been saying, the King came through Arran on the way to win his crown. That was in his dark days when everything seemed to be going against him. In after days, when he was safely and gloriously seated on his throne, he came back several times to Arran. You know how the King chose Cardross on the Clyde, between Dumbarton and Helensburgh, as his home; it was there he kept lions as pets, although they would hardly be allowed in to sit up and beg at the breakfast table. Well, from Cardross the King would take a turn down the Firth to hunt in Arran, for he was a keen sportsman. In an old account book of that time, we find that the sum of two shillings was paid to six men for taking the King's yacht over to Arran. A king nowadays would be thought a trifle mean if he gave that sum as a *tip* to his boatmen, to say nothing of wages, but, of course, a shilling was of very much greater value then than it is now.

On his hunting excursions the King would put up at Brodick Castle. His yacht and boats would ride at anchor off the little quay below the castle, which was then the only pier in Brodick Bay, and in the dewy mornings the sound of horn and the cries of the King with his knights and gillies would be heard in Glen Rosa and Glen Cloy, or on the heather hills where the red deer lived proudly and well.

When you look up to-day at the noble castle, with its walls covered with bright green ivy, you may say, "Well, now, and it was there that the great King lived!" That is the case, in a way; but the castle you see to-day is hardly the house that sheltered the King. A part of the lower wall of the main building is the only bit remaining of the castle of Bruce's time, which was destroyed in 1455. Of the rest of the building you see, part of it was built in the sixteenth century and part of it in the seventeenth. Additions to the castle were made in 1844, and at the same time the inside of it was all changed. At the right-hand end you see a low flat building: that is a battery for light guns. Formerly a tall wall and towers stood to the right of the battery, and also a tall wall to the left of the main building: these contained a great court-yard, but have been removed. The castle was protected by the steep bank in front and by a broad ditch on the north side. The tower on the left of the main building was built in 1844, but fell a year later after a great storm.

Few castles in Scotland have changed hands oftener than Brodick, and not many have so often been destroyed. Every enemy who sought out Arran, whether the English in the wars against the Scots, or the Scots themselves in their feuds with one another, made for Brodick Castle, for it was the chief fortress of the island.

There were other castles in Arran, of which you can see the ruins still. There is the castle at Loch Ranza and the castle at Kildonan. The castle of Loch Ranza was bitterly treated by the M'Allisters in 1602. Besides these castles, there were, as we have already noticed, fortified towers on Holy Isle and at Lamlash. Nothing can now be seen of that on Holy Isle, and all that remains of the Lamlash castle is a few low green mounds on the lawn of Whitehouse there.

Let me give you a few notes of the fortunes,

or rather the misfortunes, of Brodick Castle in the fierce and dangerous days of old. (1) In 1455 the Earl of Douglas sent off his kinsman Donald Balloch to harry the shores of the Firth with seventy ships and over five thousand men. They destroyed Inverkip on the mainland, and then came to Arran, slaying and burning through the island and ruining Brodick Castle. (2) During the feud in the sixteenth century between the Hamiltons and the Douglases, two Stewarts, called Archibald and Robert, sons of the Sheriff or (as we would say) Lord-Lieutenant of Bute, who supported the Douglas, seized Brodick and destroyed "the Castle and Place":—the word "Place" is first cousin to the word Palace. (3) In 1558, an English fleet under Lord Sussex set sail from Dublin and burned Kintyre and Arran, with Brodick, and then the Cumbraes. At the Cumbraes they suffered badly from a terrible tempest like the one Hakon experienced centuries before. (4) In 1646, during the Covenanting times, a raid of Campbells into Arran occurred. They laid waste all Brodick and the lands around, stealing or destroying two thousand cows. (5) In April, 1652, when Cromwell was in power throughout England and most of Scotland, one of his generals, called Major-General Deane, sent a detachment from Ayr to Arran under a certain Captain Goldsmith, who summoned the castle. It surrendered to the

Roundheads, and there they remained a good long time.

These are the main events in the history of Brodick Castle. But all the while lesser events took place which meant much to the people there and especially to the farmers and fisher-folk about, whose life for the most part must have been a harassing and perilous one.

Of the time when Cromwell's soldiers held Brodick, some exciting stories are told. For example, there is the story of the "Bealach nam Bo." That is the name of a field beside the Cnocan Burn below the Castle. It means "The Cows' Pass," and this is how it got its name. One day some soldiers from the garrison in the Castle seized upon a cow belonging to the farmer of Cnocan, and were proceeding to lead the animal away. The good farmer learned of this, and rushed to the spot, filled with rage. His wife, gentle body, tried to hold him back, for she feared the soldiers would round on him and do him a hurt. But the sturdy Highlander shook her off, and, taking his reaping-hook, slashed the cow across the legs, hamstringing her, and cried, "Better a a dead cow than nothing!"

Another day a party of these soldiers were away along the shore to the north, collecting stores for themselves about Glen Sannox, which means that they were simply taking with rude hands what the people would not give willingly. But the patience of the suffering folk in their little farms could bear it no longer. Angry words were spoken, eyes flashed, and hands were clenched, a quick blow fell, a scuffle followed, blood was shed, and straightway the whole glen was roused. Men seized their sickles, hay-forks, and anything that would serve as a weapon against the hated English soldiers, and leapt to the fight. Women called aloud, some beseeching their men folk to keep clear of it, others urging them on with fierce cries. Little children fled indoors, but the older lads hung on the edge of the battle, trembling with excitement, cheering their fathers and brothers as they fought, and themselves getting in a stroke when they could. The soldiers made a good fight of it to begin with, but their ranks were scattered and the struggle became a group of separate combats, at the gable-end of cottages, in the roadway and along it, and on the green fields above. The Highlanders fought with the courage of desperate men. They were determined to make an end of these tyrants. And an end of them they made! One by one the hated *Sassunnachs* were laid low in death. The soldiers tried to break off the conflict and escape south towards the Castle, and so the battle went straggling along the shore. It had begun at the Sword Burn, which comes down between Sannox and Corrie. The last soldier to fall crawled beneath a great boulder but was pulled out and killed. This stone is commonly called the Cat Stone, but it has nothing to do with cats. If it had to do with any animal, it would be the dog or the wolf, I think, for it was a dirty dog or a were-wolf that was slain beneath it. Truth to tell, the word Cat in the name which some people give the Stone is a mistake for the Gaelic word Cath. The stone's proper name is "Clach-a-Cath," which means the "Stone of Battle."

The story I have just told you is told by some in a different way. They say it took place on the shore below Brodick Castle, and that the Governor of the Castle himself was in the fight and managed to escape in a boat with his soldiers, but that one of them was left on shore and was chased, caught, and killed under a great boulder at Merkland Wood, near the shore-road, which is still called "Creag-an-Stobaidh," that is "Rock of Stabbing." It is a fine story either way, but it is a likelier thing to place it at Corrie, as I have done. I think the story of the Englishman killed at the Stabbing Rock goes best with what happened at the time Bruce came through Arran to win his crown.

This brings us back to Bruce, and it is time we returned to him.

I am sure you know how Bruce was crowned King of Scots at Scone in 1306, and how he was defeated at Methven Wood near Perth. Well, after that sad and treacherous battle, he fled with his companions to the Highland hills, and after many hardships and wild adventures, he got away down through Kintyre, where Angus M'Donald sheltered him and helped him greatly. He crossed to the island of Rathlin, off the north coast of Ireland, and there he rested, sometimes in great doubt, sometimes with good hope springing up in his breast. Was it not there that the little grey spider delivered her little sermon of Try Again to the downcast King? He made up his mind to pass over to Scotland again. His own earldom was in Carrick in Ayrshire, and there he resolved to go. But, first, he had to spy out the land to see if the English were there in force, and what his own men in Carrick were doing and thinking. Then it was that two of his knights proposed that they should go to Arran and find if Arran was safe for the King. From Arran, you see, he could cross straight over to Carrick, when the times were ripe. So the advance party came to Arran, and ten days later the Bruce followed. Then, in due time, the King and his tattered men sailed away from King's Cross Point to try their fortune and win freedom for the Scottish nation.

* * * * *

But all this is too long a story to be told hurriedly! Therefore we shall carry it over to a chapter by itself. You know, of course, that King's Cross gets its name from this "Crossing of the King." Long ago King's Cross went by the name of Pennycroce.

THE BRUCE: THE STORY

THE BRUCE: THE STORY

"The Tale of the King's Crossing"

I

SIR JAMES DOUGLAS and Sir Robert Boyd were walking by the shore. You would hardly think they were knights, if you looked only at their dress, for it was torn and worn. But not even the meanest beggar's rags could conceal the noble bearing of these Scottish gentlemen, their proud yet gentle manner, the flash of high and fixed resolve in their eyes. Their plaids streamed out on the wind that blew from the shore northward over the sea, as it ran glistening in gold and azure in the bright sunshine of that March morning away to the coast of Argyll. For this was the island of Rathlin on which they stood. Hither had they come with their lord and king, Sir Robert de Brus, and here they were glad to rest awhile after the terrible hardships and dangers and hairbreadth escapes they had shared with him since the black day of defeat at Methven Wood.

Behind them, where now they paused on the beach talking seriously and eagerly, there was heaped against a green bank a forlorn cottage, with as many gaping cracks in it as there were stones, and roofed with turf. A twisted tree sprawled its bare branches over the gable of it, and whin bushes, with sparkles of yellow on their spikes, huddled close to the door. Within this wretched hut lay the King on a couch of straw. His two knights had left him there in a mood of dark brooding; at times like this they found it best to leave their master to himself. In a little while he would be rid of the black fit and show so bright a hope in the future that their own hearts would kindle at it, as at a fire. That was the way of their great lord.

Said the Douglas to the Boyd: "The wind sits fair for Scotland, and I weary of this island with its foaming shores. There was a great giant once, they say, called Finn, who took this sea in one step to Kintyre and the sea of Kilbrendan in another to Arran. A ship would foot it in such a wind as this well-nigh as speedily as Finn! Come, fair Robert, let us ask licence of the King to be his ushers in Arran, whence, if the land be ready and our lord will, we will pass to Carrick and rouse the Red Lion once again!"

To this the Boyd agreed right willingly, and they prepared between them the plan they would lay before the King, when a shout from the cottage summoned them in good cheer to his presence. They found the King hoisted on one elbow on his couch, with a whimsical look upon his face.

"Did not the Lady Buchan play true to me," he cried, as they stood within the doorway; "did she not encourage my heart when she set the crown on this towsy head of mine at Scone? Behold, good knights, another lady has given manliness to my heart this day!"

Then, as the knights stood wondering how much of this was a riddle, and how much plain fact, the King went on:

"Nay, she is out of sight now, parday! Look you, somewhere yonder behind the beam. But down from that other branch the little grey lady swung into my court with her silken train, and, making due obeisance, essayed to retire to that other, where now she hides among her tiring-women! . . . Why stare you, simples, with eyes that glower like the eyes in a lanthron that a bairn hollows from a neep at Hallowe'en! 'Twas but a spider, gowks!"—and the King laughed loudly. "Once she swung to reach the other beam and failed, and again she tried and failed, and six times it thus befel, whereupon said I within my cowardly breast, 'By the saint that strengtheneth that brave heart of thine, little grey dame, essay it yet again and accomplish it, and I will essay once more to perch myself on the Scottish throne, or hold myself a craven knight!' And lo she called on her saint, and swung again and gained her throne."

The knights laughed, but not entirely as at a jest, for the King's face took on a serious look, though happy, and they knew that the ships would now be sailing soon.

"By Saint Marnock," cried the Boyd, "your arrow has a target ready for it, sire, for we have a plan to set before your grace, made on the shore a while ago, even as the little grey lady was weaving her charm."

So the two unfolded their scheme. The King seized upon it, and sent for the Lord Edward, his brother, who became King of Ireland in after days, and with quick words he cut it down here and enlarged it there, and called his knights the gentlest and doughtiest squires that ever a King had in all the world! And thus it was arranged that Douglas and Boyd should sail in advance to Arran, and make ready a place for them to take the leap across to Carrick. If no word came back to the King from Arran in nine days, he would follow them thither with the rest of their company.

As the King talked, he pulled long straws from his couch and bit upon them. He tied them into knots and tore the knots asunder, as one who would thus break through all tangles in his path. He took a withered thistle between his fingers, which pricked him. About to cast it from him, he paused and said: "Rose of Scotland! Even when dead thou woundest! Set this in my helm, Sir James. Before we die, my lords, we will work such a work in Scotland that, long after we be dead and all decayed, none shall go scatheless for evermore that tramples upon Scotland!"

II

It is the south-west wind that brings rain, and a thick drizzle began to fall as the two knights in their galley came within the shelter of the east coast of Kintyre. The breeze died away and the oars were got out. Twelve men they had aboard, ragged fellows from Ayr and Perth and Ulster, but with a loyalty in their hearts to Robert the King and his knights, which almost raised themselves to knighthood.

There was little danger of their being seen from Arran as they rowed along the western shore of Kilbrannan Sound, for the thick mist on Ben Bharran and Ben Nuis over the strait was now thickening downwards to the green plain and the water's edge. But they were taking no risks, and so they hugged the dark shore until the dusk began to gather, then the bow of the galley was flung outwards to sea and the crossing to Arran begun.

They made the other side at Machrie, and brought their little ship up the mouth of the burn, for the tide was full, and on a shingle bank, beneath a thicket of over-hanging hazel, they made her fast. The ebb-tide would leave her there high and dry, but the bushes, leafless though they were, concealed her well. The mast with its sail and tackle, the oars and the rudder, they carried up the stream and hid them snugly out of sight among the saplings of the wood.

They started without delay on their journey across the island, moving two by two with the knights at their head, and saving the time of the evening meal by munching their hard oaten cakes as they marched. Sir Robert, who knew well the island and its tracks, was guide to the little party. It was a cold and desolate way they went, through the wet woods of the plain, and then up to the black glen and through the misty passes of the hills. But these men took hardship by day and dreary journeys by night as readily as men breathe their native air, and their memory of the brave compliments which the King had made them, when they sailed from Rathlin, still burned warmly in their breast.

Before morning broke, they were swinging down Glen Sherraig to the Brodick shore, their brogues of hairy hide making as little noise as the feet of gliding ghosts. Round the bay they took their road, past the high stone [9] near the mouth of the Rosa Burn, and so by the turf above the beach until they spied the square bulk of the castle loom above them through the grey mist of dawn. Now they must go warily. Like cats of the hills they crept forward through the trees towards the great bank on which the castle stands. A halt was ordered by signs passed silently from man to man. All was quiet as the grave, save the sound of a gusty wind which awoke in the bare branches of the trees, and stirred white waves on the shore below. Scouts must be sent forward to find out what guard was being kept by the garrison. Douglas was marking the men who should go, when the sound of voices coming down the track from the castle to the shore fell upon their ears. Silently the Scots melted out of sight behind bush and rock, and waited. It was a party of a score of soldiers from the garrison, straggling down towards the sea, moving as men who would still be gladly a-bed, and muttering curses as they stubbed their toes on stone or tree-root in the path.

The Scots allowed them to pass, and then, spreading out behind them, followed them like a net to the shore. Three boats were tossing alongside the little quay. In reply to a hail from the soldiers, several men on board stood up and made ready to get out the cargo to the green stones of the wharf. Casks of flour and kegs of wine were there, and such other stores for the Castle as made the hearts of the Scots in their ambush leap up with joy, at the prospect of a good feast after a good fight. But not a sign of their presence was given until the precious stuff was all of it ranged and piled on the shore and the soldiers had begun their heavy task of carrying it up to the Castle. The sailors too bore a hand, leaving two of their number in each boat to fend her off the quay, for a fair sea was now rising from across the bay.

But they were eased of their task that day! The line of porters had strung out towards the wood on their laborious climb, when the call of a plover sounded to the right and a like call answered from the left. It was the signal of attack. Raising a loud cry of "A Bruce! a Bruce!" the Scots bounded forward and struck in upon the amazed and staggering line. Down bumped cask and keg, and here and there the good wine mingled, as soon as it spilled, with the blood of the carriers. Apart from the terrifying suddenness of it all, nothing could withstand that rush and surge and swingeing sword-play of the Scots. The English were beset as by furies from the Pit. They whipped out sword or dagger, did some of them, but their defence was slashed aside like straw, and down they went, dead men or wounded unto death. In almost as short a time as it takes to tell of it, every one of them lay still upon the path, or down against the trunks of trees, or deep within the brambles by the track.

The shouts of the attack and the cries of the fight raised an alarm in two directions. On the one hand, the men left in the boats heard the din and did their best to get their craft off and out from the quay. They loosened the hawsers and pushed with all their might; they shoved out the oars and tried to turn the boats into the wind. For a time they succeeded, but the force of the waves had now greatly increased, and two of the vessels got out of hand and came lashing broadside on the rocks, where they broke and filled. The sailors cried aloud for mercy, but, not daring to come ashore, sank and were drowned.

In the Castle, too, the alarm was sounded. The Governor, Sir John de Hastings, got him out of bed, and ordered his people to the rescue. Somewhat tardily the soldiers obeyed. They could not be sure what numbers had fallen upon their comrades among the trees below, but down they came bravely enough to do their part. The Scots, in great fettle from their victory, turned heartily up the hill against them, and carried themselves so fiercely that the English, after a show of fighting, turned tail and made for the shelter of the Castle gate. At their very heels followed the lean Scots, and several of their enemies were outstripped in the race and laid low. Up to the very threshold of the door the swift pursuers leapt, and gave up only when the large gate slammed to and the bolts were shot over with a ringing crash. One wretched soldier remained outside. With one glance at the hopeless door, he bounded away to the right, down through the wood, and sped like a hare along the shore. But a couple of determined Scots went after him as steadily and relentlessly as hounds after their prey. The man looked hither and thither as he ran for a place of refuge, and at length turned his frantic footsteps to a great rock by the way. Under it he crept, thinking his pursuers might not have seen. But only too well for him they saw! They dragged him out by the feet and finished him there.

Douglas and Boyd now collected their victorious band, and, without hindrance from the Castle, betook themselves and their plunder away. They secured the undamaged boat, and, loading it almost to the water with the spoil, rowed off across the bay to the sandy beach where the Cloy burn draws to the sea. From thence they made their way to the old fort in Glencloy,[17] and had right good cheer among themselves, with victory comforting their hearts, and Sir John's victuals comforting them otherwise. They had not lost a single man.

III

Ten days later, a fleet of thirty-three galleys came rowing cannily past Pladda and Dippin and Largie Mor, and, crossing the wide bay, rounded the Point of King's Cross, and beached themselves in the little bay within. A stalwart gillie carried the King ashore, for it was indeed the King, come to Arran from Rathlin with all his company, three hundred men in all. Stout hands were laid on the gunwales of the ships, and so were they dragged up high and dry upon the shore. A man appeared at the door of a poor hut which stood where the Pointhouse now stands. A woman joined him, and the two came down through the rocks to the sand. They showed no fear, for these new-comers, by their look, could not be English. They saw a tall knight stand a head high above a group of his chiefs, and to him they made their way.

Had they heard tell of a band of Scots in the island of recent days, asked the King. Indeed, they had! a band of knights and their men had had a bonny fight at the Castle of Brodick, and now the accursed Governor and his folk were shut up within it like rabbits with ferrets round their hole, to the joy and ease of all poor men in Arran. And where were they housed? asked the King.

The woman answered and said that as she came by Glencloy but yesterday from her dead mother at the glen-foot, there she saw the good Scots, and had hid herself at first, but needlessly, for they treated her with fair courtesy, and said, "Have no fear, mother, the wolves are caged."

At this the King rejoiced greatly, and gave the woman a silver stud from his dirk, saying, "Good friends, you shall lead me thither to-morrow morn," and they said, "Gladly, my lord; the saints bless and prosper your grace!"

The King got his people housed that night in the cottage at the Point and its little barn, and in the clachan a short way to the south along the hill-side, and they fared well, for the people of the place hailed them as their saviours, and when they learned that the tall knight was Robert the Bruce, they would have given their hands off to serve the King.

Next morning, in the brisk air and the sunshine, the King was rowed across the loch to the Kirktoun of Lamlash, and from there he climbed the steep brae over which the track went to Brodick. He and his ten companions went gently, for the woman went with them as their guide. To the summit they passed pleasantly, and before them Goatfell lifted his mighty head, covered with shining snow. To the left of the circle of standing stones [22] they walked (six feet high they stood then above the

"The King unslung his horn and blew a blast."—P. 155.

grass), and then bore off to the left towards the bosky woods that filled Glen Cloy. As they neared the glen, the King unslung from his shoulder his hunting-horn and blew a blast. The clear notes thrilled round the hills, echoing from rock to rock, and then were silent. Faintly came the call again from far along and down, like an echo of the King's call. But it was no echo. It was blown by the huntsman of the good Sir James, who, when the King's horn sounded, had jumped to his feet with the cry, "Let loose, let loose, it is the King's call!"

It was a great and merry meeting. Over the heather came streaming the men of Douglas and Boyd, the two knights heading the welcome. Glad hands were clasped, and the King smote his noble henchmen on the shoulder to commend them, as the story was told, and the men raised many a shout and mingled with one another like friends that had been parted for years. To the dùn in Glencloy they all went back, and there the night was spent.

The woman had betaken herself to her father's house at the glen-foot, with many kindly words of gratitude from the King. She would go to her aged father, she said, and join the King's party on the morrow, if she might, and go with them home to Pennycroce.

IV

The spring days went past, and still the King lingered in Arran with his followers. But the time was well spent in getting flesh on the lean bodies of his people, and having all made ready for the big adventure in Carrick over the sea. The King was the heart and soul of all their preparations. But on fitting days he would hie him away to the hill above Cnocanchoilich and the high glen of Ashdale to hunt with his merry men, and many a time they came back by Achancairn laden with their kill, with the children of the clachan capering and squealing about the happy hunters. The face of the King was the face of a man who had never a care in the world to worry him. But it wore another look in the twilight, as he talked with his knights apart: gravely then he heard reports and discussed with them his plans, and yet all the while hope shone in his eyes like a constant star.

Thus it was he looked one stilly night when he called the young squire Cuthbert to his council and gave him his chance of knighthood. Would Cuthbert pass over to Carrick with three good gillies and find how the land now lay? How stood the men of Carrick towards their lord: were the English there in strength: would he make sure of these things and the like, and, if he thought well of them, raise a beacon-light on the hill of Turnberry as a signal of good hope to his lord in Arran? Cuthbert listened well and eagerly as the King spoke, then kneeling down thanked the King with obedient words, and the King gave him his hand and said, "We will make a gentle knight of thee yet, little lad!"

So Cuthbert sailed away, and a time of anxious waiting had to be put in as well as it might. But two nights after, the King standing high on the Viking-mound at the Point, saw a faint flicker rise and fall on the far hill of Turnberry. He called his folk to witness it, and they looked stedfastly whither the King pointed. One could make out nothing; another, to please the King, avowed he saw the blaze; but many doubted. Then slowly the glimmer grew until none could remain uncertain, for it hung like a red star steadily above the sea and burned for a long while, before it died low and was no more seen.

In the warm dusk the men assembled, accompanied to the little bay by the people of the place. The blessing of heaven was called upon them as they went. The women threw packages of food upon them, the best of that day's baking, with cheerful good wishes, though some of them were sad enough, for certain of the best lads had joined the King and were sailing away from home that night. The good wife of the hut above the Point brought her two young sons to the King and besought him to have them as his men-at-arms.

"Gladly," replied the King, "if the good lads are willing."

"Your grace," said the boys stoutly, "we will follow you to h——l!"

The King laughed, but their mother cried out upon them for loose-tongued herds—

"They have their father's mouth, your grace," she went on, "but good, braw lads, for all! God keep your lordship, you will have your desire! My mother, as she died, kissed the cross and said, 'Mary, sweet one, you will help a prince to win his realm.' So she said, your grace, her with the second sight, as she was, and aye frightening folk. Even so she said, my lord King, and even so may the blessed Molaise and Donan, and Christ their lord, speed it well!"

"Amen, mother," replied the King very courteously, and, stooping down, kissed the good-wife on the brow.

The galleys were being drawn down from the shore, crunching the white shingle with their keels, and slushing over the sand to the water's edge. In waded the men, pulling them out till they floated free, and so they were brought across to the rocks, where the lading of man and gear was quickly done. Out to the open sea the oars drove the galleys, and then the sails were spread, and the great King crossed over the sea to win his crown.

We might leave the King now as he leaves our island of Arran. But a word must be added as to how he fared when he landed on the shore of Carrick. Cuthbert met him there and, falling on his knees, poured out a disturbing and alarming tale.

"Traitor!" cried the King in a rage.

"Nay, my lord, hear me!" cried the woeful lad, and the King held his peace, while Cuthbert told that it was not he who had lighted the beacon, who it was he could not tell (and indeed no one knows to this day); the English held the castle of Turnberry with three hundred men, the people of Carrick had lost much of their devotion to their absent lord, and all their cause seemed hopeless!

It was proposed that they should go back to Arran, but the Lord Edward, the King's brother, cried out that he had enough of sea-faring and hiding in the hills, and would go on with the work. The King assented. That night they attacked the English garrison, more than half of whom were billeted outside the castle. These they destroyed, while Percy trembled within. But the land was not yet ready to rise, so the King moved off to Galloway and the mountains about Glen Trool, and there he bided his time again.

His time came.

THE FAIRIES: THE GUIDE

THE FAIRIES: THE GUIDE

She is not any common earth,
Water, or wood, or air,
But Merlin's Isle of Gramarye,
Where you and I will fare.

—KIPLING.

DON'T you think it rather foolish for anyone to set up as a Guide to the Fairies: as a Guide, I mean, to help *you* to find fairies? Does anyone believe in Fairies at all now-a-days? O yes, there are still believers to be met, in lonely glens in Scotland and in Irish cabins, where folk are not quite so cock-sure of everything as is the way of people who live in towns and cities. When I was a little lad, coming year by year to Arran for the summer holidays, I had a great friend in Lum Street—do you know where that is? She was an old dame, wearing a white mutch round her dear face, with its apple-red cheeks, and her speech was as soft and sweet as the west wind on a clover field. Many a tale of old days she told me, some of them as bright and pleasant as could be, others so dark and eerie that it took all the courage I had to get across in the night, when the tales were over, from her hut to the house where I dwelt. She believed in Fairies, and when I asked her if she had seen many, she wagged her head very wisely and said, "Wheesht!" But she told me where the Fairies were to be seen, and how to prepare myself, what to do, what to take with me and what not to take, if I would see them at the cairn or on the Fairies' Knowe near Elder Kerr's house. Alas, never once did I see so much as the flick of a green mantle, or the tip of the grouse's wing the gallants among them carry in their bonnets. Something in me was certainly out of tune: of this I was sure, for my old dame knew so surely that the Wee Folk were there!

And where do they say the Fairies in Arran are to be found? The best way to get an answer to that question is to ask the old people very gently and politely about the magic places. They will likely say, "Hoot, toot!" to begin with, and pretend to have no interest in the matter at all. But if you try again and hang on to them very gently and politely, they will tell you where the magic places are. It doesn't matter very much if they say at the end, "O, it is just nonsense!"—that is what they always say! They will tell you of some green mound not very far away, like the knoll on the high road at Whiting Bay where the Smiddy Road meets it, or the Fairies' Hill in Glencloy.[17] There the Fairies live. And they live in or about all the cairns you can find, all the stone circles, and all the old stone chambers of Longheads and the *cists* of the Broadheads. They lurk beside bridges, especially if these pass over deep gullies, but in shallower places as well, beside fords with flat stepping-stones. Some glens are populous with them. Everywhere on the hills, where the water oozes through places of apple-green moss, and in wild lawns of short turf that is thick with thyme, you can see their dancing-rings. Some of these are bright green, and others are marked by patches of hard grass, which is called by the Gaelic people "pull of necessity." On the sea-shore, too, there are little mounds adorned with sea-pink where they gather, and under the very sea, beneath the blue water, there are beautiful fields and enchanted bowers, where the Fairies dwell in farms, milking their cows at evening, and breaking the silence with the sound of bells.

I am speaking of them as if they were still there. "Well, and so they are," say some people; but others have the news that the Fairies left Arran long ago, and they can tell you why they went and how they got away! I shall give you that story later on. Meantime, what you want to know next, I should guess, is, What are or what were the Fairies like, and in what ways did they show themselves, and what happened when people ran across them?

You and I are apt to think of the Fairies as very little folk. And why not, you say: do not people speak of them as the Wee Folk? And have we not all heard or even learnt by heart the poem of that gentle Irishman, William Allingham, which begins, "Up the airy mountain," and in which they are all wee folk—

"Wee folk, good folk,
Trooping all together:
Green jacket, red cap,
And white owl's feather."

But the Fairies were not all wee folk. They were of all sorts and sizes. Some of them were as great as giants; others of them were of the same size as Human Folk; many were of a shape that was partly human and partly animal. If we would know properly about the Arran Fairies, we must get this into our heads. Don't let us think of them as the dainty little creatures we see in picture-books, or in the pantomime at Christmas, or in that loveliest dream that ever was dreamed, *A Midsummer Night's Dream*. I think that the English knew only that kind of Fairy; but in Scotland and Ireland there never, never, were such Fairies! A wise man once told me that even in England such Fairies were not, till they came over from Provence in France. Mr. Rudyard Kipling, too, simply doesn't believe that the real old English Fairies were like the ones with gauze wings and very thin cloaks of green, and a silver star on a silvery stick, which we see tripping about the Babes left to die in the Wood by the Wicked Uncle! In that perfectly splendid book *Puck of Pook's Hill* —(if you are so miserable as not to have that book, you must sit down before your parents and howl till you get it!)—in that book, we meet Puck, who is quite the oldest thing in all England, and he talks with Dan and Una. Una says to Puck, "You talk about the 'People of the Hills,' but you never say 'fairies.'" And Puck replies, "How would you like to be called 'mortal' or 'human being' all the time, or 'son of Adam,' or 'daughter of Eve'?" Then Puck pours out a simply withering scorn on the people who think of Fairies as "little buzz-flies with butterfly wings and gauze petticoats, and shining stars in their hands, and a wand like a school-teacher's cane."

Well, after all that, one hardly likes to give the name of Fairy to the real Fairies at all. The name has got spoilt. It would be better for us to call them the Wee Folk, as many do; but then, as I have said, they were not all wee, by any manner of means. Or we might call them, as Puck of Pook's Hill did, the Old Things: that is a good name, as we shall have cause to see, but you must be careful always to spell the words with capital letters. Perhaps the best name to give them is "the Fay Folk": the word Fay is what the word Fairy comes from.

But now let me return to tell what the Fay Folk were like. Some of them were quite small, a few spans high. Some of these were dressed in green, some in red, some in brown. The green and brown ones went in companies together, the red singly and alone. Often they took on the disguise of little animals, like frogs or bees or hares or birds. They were light-hearted little fellows, and, as a rule, very mischievous, but the *lepracauns* among them were always working hard. The *lepracauns* were the shoemakers of the Fay Folk, and a busy life they had of it, for what with dancing and trooping over hill and stream, their shoes were always wearing out. Then there was the Hungry One, a solitary lad among them, who lingered about farm-doors on the outlook for food.

Others of the Fay Folk were as big as Human Folk, as I have told you, and others were monsters in size and shape. There were Giants among the Fay Folk, like the Giant in Scorradale (the dale of Norse Scorri), and there were wild creatures who flopped upon the roof on stormy nights, and horrible beings called the Bocans who lived in the sludge at the bottom of deep pools and came forth all oozy to the banks; and terrible things which looked like men or women till you saw a hairy hoof beneath their robe; and eerie creatures called

Bleaters, whether animal or not it was difficult to say, who went in and out of the byres with the cattle; and monsters who invaded the byres and gored the cows to death; and sleek beings called Pookas that could take the shape of horses, but woe to the man who mounted and rode them near water; and veiled phantoms with a cloak upon their headless shoulders. I tell you the Fay Folk were a horribly mixed lot! And quite as mixed was their behaviour, the things they did to people and the way they did them. Sometimes they were as kind as could be to the Human Folk, helping them in the house or in the harvest-field, leaving bannocks ready for eating, which the ploughman found at the end of a furrow, nursing the children as well as any mother could, threshing the corn for the farmer during the night, and in other ways as well doing the square thing. But even the good ones among them took the tantrums sometimes and gave all sorts of trouble. Much of it was merely mischievous, but much of it was downright bad, and some of it was wicked and horrible enough to put them in jail for life, had they been men and women of to-day. They would shoot at the cattle with their little flint arrows; many a time farmers believed their cows were suffering from "elf-wounds," as they were called. They would steal children away from home, especially little girls, and keep them in their underground houses or in their palaces beneath the sea, for ever. Sometimes young men would wander away with some lady of the Fay Folk and disappear, being seen no more, or, if he did turn up again, he was so strange that people saw he had lost his wits in the strange dwellings of Faerie. Sometimes on lonely moors or in the stony banks of streams, people at night would find a hole opened in the ground, and looking in, would see the Fay Folk making merry, singing and dancing and drinking their dewy wine. Woe betide him if he entered in: happy would he be if he escaped at all! The songs they sang were strange and magically sweet, but they were simple songs, repeating the same words over and over again. There is the famous song of the Fay Folk called "Monday, Tuesday." These were all the words of it, just "Monday, Tuesday, Monday, Tuesday." Once a man heard them sing it, and he cried out "And Wednesday." The Fay Folk were delighted to learn this addition to their chant, and as a reward they cured the man of his hump, for he was a hunch-back. Then came another hunch-back, who had heard of this good fortune, and he cried out, "And Thursday and Friday and Saturday." But this was too much for the Fay Folk. They flew up in anger and, for a punishment, clapped on his back the other man's old hump, so that ever after he went about with two.

Much more serious and often very dreadful were

the things that the monstrous creatures among the Fay Folk did. They killed men and women and cattle, breaking all the bones in their bodies and tearing the skin from the sheep dogs. They leapt behind horsemen as they rode by lonely ways and strangled them. They stretched out slimy arms from the gloomy pools of rivers and sucked down travellers to their death.

It must have been a fearsome affair getting about in those days, especially at night. But surely something could be done to protect men and women and little children and cattle from the capers and crimes of the Fay Folk? O yes, there were heaps of charms to keep oneself safe! It was wise to set out dishes of food for them, either at your own house or on the rocks beside the magical places. Oatmeal or an oatcake was a good protection. Sprinkle it on the bee-skeps, or break a cake over a child, and they were safe! When you were threshing the corn, it was wise to leave a few grains on a stone near by: that would keep the Fay Folk sweet. When a person was suffering from some strange disease, which must have been wrought by a Fay spell, kill a cock and bury it near the house or under the bed, and the spell would break. Should you fear meeting the wicked sprites or monsters, be sure to have something of iron with you, a knife, a needle or the like, because the Fay Folk are powerless against iron. If you saw them flying above you like a swarm of bees, throw an iron reaping-hook among them, and you do for them. Should you come across a poor mortal trooping with the Fay Folk as their captive, get his coat or her mantle quickly and throw it over them, and you will set the prisoner free. These were some of the magics which broke the magics of the Fay Folk.

Now isn't all this that we learn about the Fay Folk a fearful jumble? It is indeed. How *could* people come to think of all these beautiful and terrible and muddled things, and to believe in them? The answer is: the beliefs grew in a very jumbled and muddled way. And if you have a little patience, and are willing to think a bit as I go on, I can tell you in a way how the beliefs began and grew. We must go back for a little to those old Stone Age men, the Longheads and the Broadheads, of whom this book speaks in its first chapter. You know how those ancient men came in waves to Arran from the Continent. Before they started to cross from the coast of France, or thereabouts, they would see the green shores over there in England and think what a sunny land that is! And daring ones of the clan would get across, and some of them would come back and tell of the lovely lands and islands that were waiting for them, rich with nuts and wholesome roots for food and full of good hunting. So the story grew of a blessed realm in the western sea, and this story they never forgot. When they did cross over in large numbers and reached the most westerly coasts, and saw nothing but the endless ocean and no more land, the old story still stayed in their minds, and they began to believe that the blessed realm must be hidden beneath the sea itself.

These people used weapons of stone and flint, as you remember. They lived in houses underground or in mounds of stone and earth. They brewed a strange drink from the heather—

> "From the bonny bells of heather
> They brewed a drink long syne,
> Was sweeter far than honey,
> Was stronger far than wine."

They buried their dead in corridors, divided up into little "houses" under cairns, or in little single chambers, a foot or so square, to receive the ashes when they had burned the bodies. They had a religion of a kind: they believed in spirits, spirits of old hills, of rocks, of trees, of streams, some of them friendly, others of them wicked and harmful. To these spirits they made offerings of food, flesh, and grain. They had special religious rites, at midsummer, and on November eve and on May eve.

The Broadheads, you remember, knew the use of bronze. But greater by far than the discovery of bronze, was the discovery of iron. It was as great a discovery to ancient man as the discovery of steam or electricity was to us. A man with an iron weapon could face almost any enemy. For fighting wilder men who were armed with stone or bronze weapons, iron was almost a miracle of strength. And this memory of the perfectly wonderful power which iron gave, lingered on in the minds of men, and so when they wanted something to guard them against invisible enemies as well, such as the Fay Folk, they turned to iron—anything of iron, a knife, a needle, for safety.

In course of time, the Gaels came to Arran. They conquered the Old Race of Arran they found there, killing many of them, making slaves of some, and chasing the others up into the hills and the high glens and the lonely shores of the sea and the rivers. They saw the Old Race making offerings of corn and meal to the spirits and ghosts of streams and woods and stones, and holding strange festivals at midsummer and the like, and the Gaels thought these were proper things to do, for they too believed in those spirits and ghosts, and so they did the same. Those of the Old Race who were enslaved, the Gaels made work for them in the fields and about the house, sometimes even as nurses for their children. Silent, huffy, mischievous helpers they made, but often they were as devoted as dogs to their new masters. But the prouder ones of the Old Race lived their own life as of old on the high borders of the farms of the Gaels. Sometimes a Gaelic farmer would smell cooking near the field as he ploughed. It came from an underground house of the Old Race he had not known was there! He would draw near to examine it, and the old earth dwellers would give him a bannock to keep him sweet. Or at night a Gael, coming over the hill, would see a hole in the ground, as he thought it was, full of light! Forward he would go, to find a company of the Old Race making merry within their mound, all of them in jolly fettle except one who had so much to do in keeping their shoes of untanned hide in good repair that he hadn't time for junketing. But he made up for it, for he gathered a good "bag of gold" for his labours. Now and then a kindly Gael would have a try at winning the proud Old Race to the life and ways of the Gaels. He would join them in their home and teach them a little of his own higher wisdom. A good thing to start with was the names of the days of the week. And the men of the Old Race were willing enough to learn, but slowly! One new thing at a time was enough, and it was amusing; they could sing it like a little song. But should the teacher try to burden them with too much, he became a nuisance; the earth people would arise and beat him off, raising a lump on his back as a warning for the future. Sometimes, too, a venturesome young man of the Gaels would meet in a woodland place a girl of the Old Race, and falling in love with her, forsake his own people, and go off with the people of his bride in their hidden homes. Such an one would be looked upon by his own clan as dead and gone.

But the proud people of the Old Race found life becoming hard and harder still. They began to die off. Then they took to stealing the children of the Gaels, especially the little girls, who would grow up as mothers among them. Women of the Old Race who lived as slaves in the huts of the Gaels, joined in plots with those in the hills, and disappeared thither with the babe in their charge. Many an angry search among the hills was made by the bereaved parents and their friends; fights took place around and within the mounds; and sometimes the child was found again, weak and asleep, but sometimes it had disappeared for ever!

The Old Race found themselves in a poor plight. Hungry ones would haunt the cottages of the Gaels, begging at the door if they were brave enough, or waiting around to steal if they got the chance. And the Gaels, to save themselves from these hungry thieves, would leave out food for them at night, thinking thus to buy them off.

Gradually they disappeared. Perhaps the last the Gaels saw of them was some old man, hoary and bent, who lingered long in his round hut on the hill—

> "High on the hill-top
> The old King sits;
> He is now so old and gray
> He's nigh lost his wits."

They died out and *when they died, they became Fay Folk!* When I say they became Fay Folk, I mean that they became so in the memories and minds of the Gaels. With the Gaels the memory remained of a strange people, sometimes kindly, sometimes dangerous and uncanny, who lived underground and deep in glens and river gullies, and high in hills, who did the things I have just been describing in connection with the Old Race. They were no longer seen, but things happened from time to time which made people sure they were still about. Children were lost in the glens or on the shore, and no more seen, and no one could explain their disappearance. Young men hunting solitary on the hill, or coming over the bleak moor at night, lost their way, fell into holes and were hurt, and sometimes seen no more, or, if found, were disordered in their mind for a long time. What could explain these things? Nothing; unless it was the strange Folk of the Hills. Thus the Old Race lived on in the imagination and fears of the Gaels, and the stories lived on too, about underground dwellings full of light and feasting, and the *lepracaun* making shoes, and of children kidnapped, and young men wooed away by fay maidens, and of fairy songs about "Monday, Tuesday," and of gold hoards in houses beneath mounds, and of bannocks laid out as an offering to lonely ploughmen, and all the rest of it! And corn was left for the Fay Folk and milk on the window-sill.

The Gaels remembered in a vague way that the Old Race had to do with the cairn graves, the little chambers in corridors and in *cists,* and also with the great stones standing alone or in circles. They looked into the little chambers and *cists* and said, "These must have been their dwelling-houses," and so they came to think of them as very little people, "wee folk," a few spans high. But such wee folk could not have raised those huge stones! No, no: these must have been the work of great men; and so the belief grew that some of the Fay Folk must have been giants. And the Gaels continued to believe that there were spirits and ghostly beings about the rivers and the trees and the rocks, to whom they still made offerings. They mixed up these in their thoughts of the other strange Old Things, and these too became Fay Folk. There were old monsters among these, it is true; but the worst monsters came into their thoughts in another way. They came from *the Norse.* You remember how the Norse Vikings came to Arran and were inhabitants and lords of it for more than three hundred years. They brought their own weird beliefs, many of them as wild and terrible as one would expect from a people who came from a wild country like Norway. They believed in awful Giants, and in monsters that lurked in pools, and in Odin's dreaded night-horse. They believed in hooded phantoms without heads, a dreadful belief which began with their old savage custom of cutting off the heads of the slain, in case the dead men should haunt them. They believed in horrible beings that did wickedly in the byres, and less horrible creatures that went slinking along among the herds. These stories from the Vikings and others like them, the Gaels turned over in their minds and mingled them with their own, and thus the Fay Folk received a crowd of new recruits, which got so mixed up with the others, that men at last could not tell whence they came.

Even when the Gaels became Christians, and long after, they went on believing in the strange world of the Fay Folk. The priests of Holy Church set their faces against it all, but not very successfully. They told the Gaels that the Fay Folk were fallen angels, not the angels who were cast down to the Pit when the angels in heaven rebelled against God, but less wicked ones, some of them indeed almost innocent, who got pulled into the plot, and then dragged down with the really bad ones, when they were hurled forth from the skies! These were allowed to remain in earth and about the earth, half-way to the realm of dreadful punishment underneath.

In time the power of the holy men of Mother Church grew so great, and the blessings they uttered so many and so strong, and the sound of their bells so full, and the cocks on their steeples so bold, that the Fay Folk, or the greater part of them, left Arran for good, both "giants, trolls, kelpies, brownies, goblins, imps; wood, tree, mound, and water spirits; heath-people, hill-watchers, treasure-guards, good people, little people, pishogues, lepracauns, night-raiders, pixies, nixies, gnomes." . . . Well-a-day! and so they flitted out of Arran. But some of the old people shake their heads when they hear that, and look over their shoulders and say, "It is mebbe so, and again perhaps no, I'll be thinkin'!"

THE FAIRIES: THE STORY

THE FAIRIES: THE STORY

"Tales of the Fay Folk"

I

FAIRIES ABOVE GROUND

ONCE upon a time a farmer and friend were driving in a cart from Lamlash to Brodick. The good grey horse put down his head bravely as he pulled the cart up the big brae from the shore, and blithely the two men within cracked of horses and crops and the flavour of the grand stuff in the Ship Inn. Anon they came to the top of the hill, and the grey horse lifted up his head and eased the collar on his neck, and breathing thankfully, made a show of trotting cheerfully along. All went well till they were passing by the strange stones [22] that lie to the right of the road, an eerie place, faith, to be at in the mirk, but it was still day-light, and the stones and the green grass about them seemed empty and world-like. When what should happen, do you think, but this: the grey horse stopped, as if he had gone slap on a dry-stone dyke, and there he stood shaking with fear and snorting noisily. Now what could it be at all that gave him this fright and sweat? The farmer looked on this side, and the friend looked on that side, and the farmer stood up in the cart and looked between the horse's ears, but never a thing they saw!

Said the friend, "If I would be saying it whatever, it will be staggers Grey Robin will be having!" "Hoots away, I never!" said the farmer, and brought down his hazel stick with a sound smack on Robin's back. With a groan like an old man in pain, the grey horse bounded on, and never before did he make so fair a show at a gallop as he did that day! The cart went bumping and rattling at his tail, until at long last he got down to his even four feet, and from a trot fell to a walk. Then the two looked back along the road, and when the stour had gone down, what do you think they would be seeing? It is the truth to say that they saw a great company of little brown men on the road and hanging on to the tail-board of the cart, and, even as they looked, the wee folk loosed the tail-board and dang it down with a clatter on the ground. Then off they went in great glee, holding their little fat sides, like folk that have heard the greatest joke in the world. . . . Very soberly the farmer and the friend stopped the cart and set the tail-board on again, and drove gravely down the brae to Brodick.

Once upon a time, Archie M'Millan was driving home in his cart from the mill at Monamor in

Lamlash, to Whiting Bay. The day was dusky when he passed by the gamekeeper's above the loch and the pine-wood that is there. But the road is clear and open along the hill, and Archie had no thought in his head of anything but his own fireside and the good porridge that would be steaming beneath his nose when he got home. However that may be, he told me that some bird hooted in the pine-trees as he went past. It might be an owl, or a wild doo it might be, but it was an uncanny note it gave, and Archie flapped the reins on the mare's back, and the mare put her best foot foremost.

Now there is an eerie bit on the road further on, as you may know, and that is, to be sure, where it goes down the brae to the stone bridge over the Achancairn Burn. Maybe you have climbed up the parapet and seen the little maiden-hair ferns growing on the grey face of the bridge, and far below, the black water and the glistening rocks. Well now then, down the brae came Archie, and the light of day faded away as he came down to the dark bridge. He told me he was as sure as a gun that something would happen in that very same place, but on he went, for he was as brave as a lion at most times, although this was a by-ordinary time. When lo and behold, the mare stopped dead! And would anything make her go on?—no! She would not budge, though Archie coaxed her, and then said two or three good curses on her, and tugged the reins, and brought down his whip upon her. And I would say, Little wonder she would not budge a bit, but stood there in a quake and a cold sweat; for there on the bridge before his eyes, Archie saw a light that could be no earthly light or heavenly either, for it was a quiet blue flame like a corpse-light. Forbye that, which was terrible enough, a pale figure stood by the light, like a maiden in form and winsome enough in shape, but of a deadly beauty. Archie told me he felt the cold fear creep up his backbone and stand up his hair like bristles. But he was as brave as a lion even in this horrible plight, and though his mouth was as dry as a kiln, he was able to cry out, "On I will go, I tell ye, though I drive horse and cart to the Bottomless Pit!" and he laid on the mare with his whip when he cried it.

Upon that very word, out went the light, just as if you had puffed out a candle, and the Fay maiden melted away like a puff of mist over a dyke on the hill. On went the mare with Archie, and he was panting for breath and trembling from head to heel, not knowing what would happen at the very bridge itself. However, no evil befel them at all, as they hastened past, you will be glad to know. But he told me that just as he got round the bridge to the left, he heard a splash in the burn far down below, like the sound of a great monster slipping back again into the water.

II

FAIRIES UNDER GROUND

Once upon a time, a party of douce folk were making very merry, singing the good Gaelic songs, and dancing the good Highland dances, and joking freely and laughing and daffing, as is the way with good friends everywhere. There had been a wedding that day, and that was the meaning of the occasion. Now the whisky that night had no corks in its bottles, and the bottles were oftener on their sides than standing up quiet and still, and one by one they lay down with their last drop drained away. Well anon, said some one, "It will be needed for some one to be going to the inn at Lagg Water for more of the same!" So two of the men wound their cravats about their necks and pulled their bonnets upon their heads and, cleeking arms, the one in the other, off they set for the inn.

Within the inn the bright light of the big lamp fell in a blaze upon their eyes, and they blinked for a bit; but yonder was the good landlord smiling upon them, and here and there a cronie taking his dram quietly and talking of all things. They said to the two that came in, "Well now, and it will be dry work certainly!" and they said, "Have ye them well beddit?" and they said, "It will be elders' hours presently indeed!" and other such things. They joked together for a time, and then Alec and John opened the door, and the light shone on the road like a broad carpet of fairy gold, and out they went with the wee brown jar safe and snug between them.

Well anon, along the road they went, but cannily, for the light of the big lamp was still in their eyes, and it filled the dark before them with what looked like round lanterns that changed from green to red and back again. Then it is the truth to say that a fay thing happened. At the side of the road where the brackens hang over the bank and a bit of whin is growing, they saw indeed a hole opened, and inside the hole all was as light and bright as if a dozen lamps and more, like the lamp in Lagg inn, were burning away in one blaze. And forbye, it was like a palace inside, with Fay Folk leaping and dancing and having the high jinks, the highest you could think. The Fay Folk saw the two glowering on them from the road-side, and they gave them a wave of the hand and cried to them to come in ben and join the fun. John gripped his neighbour tight by the arm, and said in a whisper below his breath, "No, faith, catch me!" But Alec shook off his hand and said, "I will be with you, bonny birds!" and in he jumped without more ado, and there John saw him going round in the fling, cleeking and hooching with the best of them, and the wee brown jar slung on his back.

Well then, and what would John be doing but going off in a great swither to the house to tell them of these doings, and where Alec and the whisky were gone. In at the door he came with a face as white as a sheet, and with a tongue that could hardly speak a word for the trembling he was in. But they got it all out of him at the end, and out of doors into the dark they all come together, one carrying a lantern and many of them sticks, and all of them wondering what to goodness they would be finding at the hole of which John was telling them. But when they came to the place, what was there to be seen, do you think, but nothing at all whatever! Let them search where they might, not a token was there of the cavern that had swallowed up the man. The loss of the whisky was bad enough in all conscience, but even that was nothing to the loss of the man.

Then in the daytime, when the fay night was past, heads began to shake as they gossiped together, and eyes began to look agley at John, poor man, and havering women and then steady-minded men began to ask whether or no, it might be, that John had dealt Alec his death, and then made up this bogey tale to put folk off the scent of the foul murder. Aye, and they took hold of him and said, "Maybe, John, you have his body hid away, when you were done quarrelling and killing him?" But an old woman who was a spae-wife without doubt, cried out, "Take thought before you do aught till him! Do you let a year and a day pass by, before you do aught to him at all!" And the people knew she was a wise wife and they said, "A year and a day then!"

Well anon, a year and a day went by, and that day night they forgathered at the magic place of which John swore, with an oath, that there his neighbour had leapt in to dance with the Fay Folk and was no more seen. And lo and behold, there was the bright hole opened up, and inside the dancing was going on and the highest jinks you could imagine. And it is the truth to say that there was the man, jigging away in the merry-go-round of the dance, with the shoes all worn off his feet.

"Ochone, Alec, my dear," cried John, "come away to your own folk like the good lad!"

And Alec gave a wave of his hand and said, "A minute or two till I finish the reel!"

In a minute or two he finished the reel, and he stepped out safe and sound, and in a clap the ground closed for ever and a day. Now would you believe it, but Alec would believe nothing at all, but that he had only been with the Fay Folk for the time it takes to dance one reel!

Once upon a time, there was a certain old man of the name of Fullarton, and he had a way with him in knowing the Fay Folk. Close by Corriegills, in the Black Hill there (Dun Dhu), he had found a cave where a band of them had their dwelling, and away to them would he go, not once or twice but often, to have a crack and pass the time of day with them. These wee folk had plenty of gold with them, and I wonder if the old man had an eye on that, it may be. Howsomever, there would he go, and the wee folk were right pleased to see him, and had him in bye to sit with them and talk, as I have told you. There he would be a good long while, hearkening to their gossip and putting in a word himself, and knitting a stocking himself of wool of a fine heather mixture.

Aye, but he had to keep an eye about him, for many a time he saw the wee folk saunter round by the door of the cave with a look on their faces which meant they would make him a prisoner if they could. But they never managed it, and do you know why? He was wise and never was he without a darning-needle in the collar of his coat, where a man sticks the pins he finds, or else he would have a sprig of rowan about him, for the Fay Folk never bother a body that has anything of iron about him, or bonny rowan berries or even the leaf of it. Once he forgot to have these charms with him, and he had his own to do to escape from their clutches. He looked up and saw the cave was closing before his very eyes, and the wee folk drawing in on him in a ring like bairns in the game "Warning, warning, three times warning!" although never a warning they gave him, I'm thinking. Up he got and was out of the cave helter-skelter before you could say "Thief." I tell you, he stood there with the sweat on his face and his knees knocking. Aye, it was a near one that, and he learned a lesson that day he never forgot to his dying day!

III

GIANTS AND MONSTERS

Once upon a time, there lived in Scorradale Glen a fearsome Giant, who went by the name of Scorri. He was so big that I will not tell you how big he was for fear you would say, "I will not be believing that!" Well, at any rate, he was a monster in size and as fierce and dangerous as he was big. When the women would be bringing their eggs and butter into Lamlash on fine mornings, down the hill would come Scorri, with a scowl on his face and a great club in his right hand, and the boulders would go flying before his feet like pebbles before a shepherd. And the women would drop their eggs and butter where they were, and kilt themselves and run like ducks down the road to Loch-an-Eilean. Then Scorri would pick up the baskets and off with them to his den, and there suck the eggs, dozens of them, and eat up the butter, kail-blades and all! Sometimes, too, he would kill the lambs and eat them raw, and many a time the shepherds were well-nigh greeting at the losses of the lambs and the ewes as well. But they could do nothing against the Giant, and the bravest dogs they had were as weak as water when they heard him shouting on the moor.

This went on and on, till the women would come no more to Lamlash, and the butter went to waste and the eggs went bad, and they said loudly, "Are there no men left in Arran to take the road against Scorri?" The men hung their heads when they heard talk like this, but at last it got beyond bearing and they said, "There is only one way of it!" So they met together and took swords and hay-forks with them, and off they marched to try a fall with the muckle Giant.

There was a man among them with his head on his shoulders, and he made up a plan, as you shall hear in a minute. He split up the men into two parties, and he put one set of them on the one hill-side, and the other on the other hill-side, with the deep gully of the glen between them. Then the one side set up a shout and began to cry, "Scorri, ye old sinner, come on and show your courage, you that scare none but women!"

At this Scorri came tumbling out of his cave in no end of a rage, and gnashed his teeth till it sounded like the clapper of a mill. He saw the folk on the hill mocking him, and up he went to wipe them out with his club. It was a stiff climb he had, and he puffed and blew with it like a smiddy bellows. Well now, just as he got to them and was thinking of getting to work with his club, the men on the other side of the glen set up a great shout and began to cry to him, "Hey, Scorri, ye old coward, away with you and put on your petticoats, you're no man at all!" With that Scorri turned round in a bigger temper than ever, and down the hill he came with a hop, step and jump, and began to climb the other side to come at these new torments. And more than ever he puffed and blew like a wheezy bellows by now, and the wind went out and in of his dry mouth like a breeze in a wood that is bare in winter. So it was that when he reached the top where the men were ready for him, he was as weak as water, and leaned on his club to get his breath.

You will see that that was the plan of the men, for with a yell they fell on him, and many a good dunt they gave the old rascal before he could guard himself. Down the brae they pushed him till they reached the burn, and the men from the other hill came down like a torrent and joined in the game with a will. My faith, it was no game at all for Scorri! He was down on his knees by now and roaring like a bull, and the blood coming out of his nose like a burn. "Here's butter for you!" cried the men as they struck him, and some heaved stones at him and said, "Here's a bit egg for you, you old cateran!" And so Scorri died, and a very good riddance too!

Once upon a time, a farmer was riding home upon his horse by the road that runs from Lamlash up the Glen of Monamor. Now that is a lonely dale at all times, and the burn runs deep between the rocks, and the pools are dark and eerie. Much more lonely forbye it is when the light fades from the top of the Ross and the black night fills up the glen. The sky turns pale green, and that too grows black, and the only light thing is the dusty road climbing up and up, and even that grows misty and dim.

It was like this as the farmer rode upwards, thinking of his home over the hill and far away. Suddenly he felt something leap up behind him and take a seat at his back on the horse. All he knew was a sound of footsteps soft as pads upon the road, and then the Thing behind him at his back. The horse became all frantic, trembling in every limb, and stretching himself out to a wild gallop. As suddenly as before, the Thing behind him leapt off and padded softly along for a little, and then the sound of it passed away. The farmer said a thankful bit of prayer to his Maker, although still the cold ran in his blood, and he thought his heart would beat a hole in his ribs, when, good life! didn't it all happen again! Pad, pad, pad came the soft flat steps, and up the Thing leapt behind the poor man, and off went the horse in a trembling frenzy once more. He put his hand behind him to feel it, and what he felt made his flesh grue. The Thing was cold and slimy. It had hair upon it too, like an animal's hair, but he touched an arm and shoulder like the body of a human being. Back he drew his hand in horror, and lo, the Thing leapt off again, and the sound of it died away.

Indeed now, he was a brave man, the farmer, as you shall hear: for he said, "I will get to the bottom of this, if I have to suffer for it!" and he undid a leather belt he had about his waist, and made ready for the beast if it came again.

Come again it did! But now the farmer turned him in the saddle and gripped the Thing. He found it had hands like human hands, but with webs between the fingers, and hair like an otter's on the back of them. Quick as light he buckled the strap about the monster's hands, saying, "Keep you quiet now, we will have a look at you, by and by!" The beast whimpered like a bairn but kept quiet enough, and so they came to the farmer's home. He took the beast into the barn and there he tied him to a good strong post, and went in to tell his wife, and have a drop of whisky to steady himself. But hardly had he taken so much as a sip and had said to his wife, "Lod sakes, woman!" when they heard a shuffling and a bleating and a sniffing at the foot of the door, something like a dog scratching and whining to get in, and something like a cow blowing in the grass as she feeds. The farmer said, "The beast is loose, I'm thinking!" And taking a big swallow at his glass, he cried out by way of a joke like, "Away with you now and go home to your mother!" when a voice spoke behind the door, as sad as the cry of a curlew. And this is what it said—

"My beard is cold and wet,
Give me back my pet,
Give me back my bairn,
Or I'll turn thy house to a cairn!"

Lod sakes, it was the very mother of the monster! The farmer turned white now, but up he got and went out by the back door, and slipped into the barn and let loose the young monster. In the dark he heard a cry like the sound a mare makes upon her foal, and then the sound of a padding down past the dung-hill and away to the road, and the farmer came to his wife and said, "It's the church for me and you on Sabbath, I'm thinking!"

IV

FAIRIES OF THE SEA

Once upon a time, a little maid was walking in the high fields above Whiting Bay. It was in the summer-time, and the sunshine lay like gold on the windy trees and the fields and the hedges with roses and fuschias in them, and it was like molten gold on the rippling sea. The hills were like opals for colour, blue and yellow and green, and the coast of Ayr was clear as clear could be. The bees were tumbling about the white clover, and the smell of it was like honey in the warm air. The little maid found blue hare-bells growing on a mound, and these she plucked to make a posy, and a little bunch of heather with pale purple bells she plucked to keep them company, and then she took creamy clovers as well, ones with long stalks, and added them as well. And she buried her little brown nose in the lovely bunch and drew in all the fragrance of it in one long breath. Even as she did so, she lifted her brown eyes and looked away to the sea; and she looked again, and her look became a stare, for lo and behold, the sea had disappeared and was no more there. Instead of the sea all blue and gold to Ayrshire, she saw a beautiful country laid out before her gaze. Fields were there, greener and sweeter than any this earth can show, and flowers grew in heaps, and tall trees waved gently in a soft wind. Little streams, as blue as the blue sky, wound about in meadows sprinkled with roses and powdered with meadowsweet, and little cows stood up to the knees in the silvery water at the edge, some brown as rowans and others white as a seagull's breast. Smoke of the colour of a dove's wings went up from little houses with roofs that were ruddy and green like heather, and walls the colour of milk. And on the quiet wind there came floating the sound of little bells, golden bells, such as sound in the music we hear in summer dreams. Never was seen so fair and heavenly a country as that little maid beheld that day, lying like an island in the channel of the sea.

She gazed and gazed and gazed, and within her heart she began to say, "I must set my feet agoing and run to it away!" when lo, she felt her arm being taken firmly by some one's hands. In great anger she turned to see who would thus stay her from going, and there was an old woman at her side, with a crooked back and a crooked nose that almost met her chin, and crooked fingers, and she carried a crooked staff.

"Little dear one," said the old woman, "what will you be seeing in the ocean yonder, that you look as in a dream?"

"Little mother," said the little maid, "I am seeing a land that must be heaven, I am very sure, and the little cows and the little houses with the blue smoke at their chimneys," and so she began to tell the wonderful sights that there were.

But suddenly the old woman snatched away the posy the little maid was holding to her bosom, and straightway the lovely land vanished and was gone, and there was nothing in sight but the old sea, rippling in blue and gold away to the clear coast of Ayr. O very angry was the little maid as she turned to speak her mind to the old wife, but the old wife had vanished too, for she was a witch! Then, when the little maid looked on the ground, there lay the hare-bells and the heather of her posy, but the clovers were all gone. And do you know why? They had among them the magic clover which, if you hold it in your hand, gives you the sight that sees the land of the Fay Folk under the sea, which in Arran is called Innis Eabhra, and elsewhere Hy Braisil, and in Ireland Tìr-nan-Og.

Once upon a time, a crofter in the south of Arran was crossing the rocks upon the sea-shore, when he lighted upon a lady of the Fay Folk of Innis Eabhra under the sea. There she was lying asleep between two sunny rocks. Beside her lay her mantle, which was made of white swan feathers, very beautiful to see. And the lady was so sweet and fair that the man fell in love with her then and there, and made up his mind to take her to his home. But first he took her mantle of white swan feathers, for if you do that and keep it away from them, those wonderful maidens of the sea must abide with you and cannot go back to their proper home beneath the waves.

When he had got her mantle safely, he awoke her, and at first she was frightened and wept, but seeing that her mantle was taken and that the man was a handsome lad with a kind face and a clear blue eye, she followed him home quite readily and pleasantly. Indeed so content was she that the two were married as husband and wife, and two bairns were born to them, a baby boy and then a baby girl.

Thus seven years passed by, and you would think that the sea-lady had forgotten all about Innis Eabhra for ever. But ah, not so quickly do people forget their home. One Sabbath day the man betook him to the church and his sea-wife stayed behind to mind the house. Presently in come the bairns to her, saying:

"Mother, dear one, will you be coming to see the lovely thing that lies hidden beyond the chaff in the barn?"

With her heart in a flutter, off flew the sea-lady to see what this thing might be. Ah, there it lay, her stolen mantle of white swan feathers!

"Little ones," she said, "come with me and I will be kind to you."

So she gave them white bread for a treat, and new butter to it and honey of the heather-bees as brown as amber. And while they settled to so great a feast, she slipped away to the shore, and, putting on her mantle of white swan feathers, dropped gently into the deep sea opposite the Iron Rock at Corriecravie, and so went home.

But sometimes back she would come again to the croft where her husband and her two bairns dwelt. Aye, and people have seen her sit with them, combing her hair and singing them songs. One day the little son went away with her to Innis Eabhra between the waves and was seen no more. But the little daughter would not go, and was with her father till she grew up and got married, and lived happily ever after.

V

THE FLITTING OF THE FAIRIES

Once upon a time a smack set sail from Arran to the Irish shore. She was a good sea-boat and well-trimmed, and the weather was fine and a grand breeze blowing. So the sails were set and she began to draw beautifully, and her nose was edged round to the south, and her bow gathered a white bone in its mouth, as the sailors say, and everything promised well for a speedy and happy voyage.

Something went wrong! The smack grew sluggish in her pace, and, worse than that, she sailed lower in the water than she did at the start, lower and lower still, till at length the skipper and his crew began to fear that she would founder altogether and all go to the bottom of the sea. They turned themselves about to find the cause of this strange fortune, but nothing they could think of could explain it. She was dragging nothing astern, no mass of wreckage or sea-wrack; she showed no bubble or ooze of a leak within. The sailors were at their wits' end, when one of them, who had the "second sight" came up to the skipper and said in a whisper:

"There is a stranger on board! Over yonder I see a wee brown man by the bow."

The skipper looked, but not a thing could he see. Then the sailor said:

"Look you, do you this: set the soles of your feet upon my feet and stand thus, and take another keek at the starboard bow!"

The skipper did this droll thing and behold, the eyes almost dropped out of his head at the sight he saw. Everywhere, above and below, and fore and aft, on the mast and around to the very truck, and along the gaff, and on the mainsail and on the jibs, and out the bow-sprit, and along the bob-stay, and on all the stays and halyards, and over all the deck and in the hold, and on the gunwales, and on the tiller and down the rudder to the water's edge—were sitting and hanging and swinging and swaying and clutching and sprawling and huddling, hundreds and hundreds of little wee bodies of the little wee Fay Folk, red ones and green ones and brown ones, and all!

"May such a blessing as you want be upon you, little good people," said the skipper, addressing them. "But how will this be, and what if ye sink my boat?"

Then the wee folk answered and said that they had so much of blessings in Arran, they could abide it no longer, blessings, that is, of holy Christian folk. And so they were flitting! But let the captain and his men have no fear, they would all get to Ireland safe and sound. Even so it fell out, to the comfort of all.

SHIPS AND SMUGGLERS: THE GUIDE

SHIPS AND SMUGGLERS: THE GUIDE

"*And there was sailing of long galleys past her.*"
—CAEILTE'S SONG (*Silva Gadelica*).

ARRAN has always been a land of ships and their anchorage. I could wish that some great person would get up a Pageant of the Ships of Arran, not a little affair, mind you, like the models of ships, ancient and modern, which they floated on the river Kelvin at the Glasgow Exhibition in the year 1911. No, not that, but a big affair with full-sized models, which would assemble in Whiting Bay and come sailing round King's Cross Point into Lamlash Bay and out again at Clachlands Point, and then round to Brodick, where the Lady Graham would stand and graciously take the salute, and the Lord Graham would make a speech, like the gallant sailor he is. Of course, the whole business would mean a good deal of bother and some money, and you and I would think twice before we took it in hand. But I tell you it would be a great sight! You and I, to be sure, would have to be at Brodick to see the fleet giving the salute. If it weren't for that, we'd stand on King's Cross Point or on the shore at Hamilton Rock, and see close at hand from there the Pageant of the Arran Ships. We should have plenty of time to feast our eyes, as they say, on each squadron as it went past in state, for the vanguard of the fleet would be the canoes of the savage sailors of the Stone Age paddling along in their tree-trunks, hollowed by fire and flinty axes, and these, of course, cannot do very many knots an hour! Down they would bend to their crooked paddles, and you and I would say, "If that old beggar paddling stroke would only lift up his hairy face a bit, we might be able to see whether he is a Longhead or a Broadhead!"

Then come the *churraichs,* which means the boats and little ships made of wooden frames and covered with hides. Look at their brown woollen sails, and the tall Gael with his steering-oar trying to edge her off the wind a bit: mighty difficult they are to steer, those *churraichs!* And see that little group of monks standing forward in the second little ship, with what looks like red leather packets clasped to their hearts, and tall curved staves in their hands: that must be what the blessed Columba, or the holy mariner Brendan, and their companions looked like when they sailed to the western isles from Ireland, or came round past Sanda on their way to Arran.

But now what are these long craft behind them with the great striped square sails and the——why, of course, these are the dragon-ships of the Vikings! See the dread figure-heads curved above the bows, like a swan's neck, but with horrible serpents' heads, their mouths bristling with fangs, their eyes monstrous in black and white. And the coloured shields along the sides, and the great oars working like the legs of a centipede between them, and the Norse warriors standing up in their winged helmets and their red cloaks, as they do in a frontispiece of the *B.O.P.* I wish they would stop a bit till we see more of them. But on they move very stately and dangerous looking, and after them come so many kinds of ships, that one gets a little mixed in trying to make them all out.

But look! those ones rigged something like a brig but with high fo'castles and high poops, and the three leopards on their flag, these must be the English ships that prowled about the firth from time to time in the old English wars! And those black ships with tawny sails, a little like the coal boats to whose sides the carts and horses go down to-day on the Arran beaches, these are the vessels that used to trade between Arran and the ports in Ayrshire. Some of them have kegs on board which the sailors try to cover up. Bless me, these must be the Smugglers, no less! Yes, I think so, for there go the frigates of the old kings we got from Hanover and the revenue cutters of Queen Anne. And see that one with the group of men on board whose hands are tied! That must be a press-gang ship with its haul of lads for the King's Navee, caught and taken in the Arran glens—a bad time that, when the party of man-o'-war's men with their pig-tails and cutlasses went prowling through Arran after them, and the lads used to hide on the moors all night to escape them.

But do look at that brig there with its swarm of Arran people on board, men, women, and children! That is the brig *Caledonia!* We can't afford the time to-day to tell all that story as it deserves, but let me give you its outline. On the 25th of April, 1829, that ship lay on Lamlash Bay, and twelve families of Arran folk went on board, with tears in their eyes, and yet with a good brave hope shining behind their tears. They were emigrants to Canada. Changes had taken place in the way in which farms were let and run in Arran. These changes began in the year in which Waterloo was won. Formerly the people worked the farms in groups, groups of families and friends, but now each farm or piece of a farm was given to individual tenants. Small farms were swallowed up in larger farms. In one instance land which had twenty-seven families on it was made into a single farm. Fields were turned into sheep-runs. And thus many people had to seek a means of livelihood elsewhere. Especially was this the case with the cottar folk. In North Sannox a little township disappeared. During these years of change more than four hundred people emigrated, chiefly from Sannox. The Duke of Hamilton, the chief landlord in the Island, was kinder than others in the way he dealt with those exiles. But it was a woeful exodus into the wilderness beyond the ocean for these children of Arran. The party that went by the *Caledonia* held a service on board before they set sail, and the minister, the Rev. A. MacKay, preached to them on the text, " Casting all your care upon Him, for He careth for you." Away they sailed, and two months later reached Canada. They were joined there by four families of Arran people who came out later in the ship *Albion,* and they settled in Megantic County, which is fifty miles south of Quebec. There they suffered hardships enough, but the spirit of the Gael carried them through, and they succeeded in making a happy settlement of it, where their descendants still prosper.

But hold on a minute: we have so let our thoughts wander far away over the Atlantic Ocean that we almost missed that great galleon going past out there beyond the others. What can it be with its high castle at the stern and the banners flying from the bowsprit and the great lantern swinging above the poop? Is not that the flag of old Spain streaming from the mast-head? It is all so shadowy: but ah, I know that ship! It is the ship of the Great Armada which sailed past Clachlands long, long ago, and the people of the place had no cannon to fire at her, so they carried out the old witch-wife of Clachlands from her hut, that she might raise a storm, or put a good round curse on her, with her spells. But she didn't. And why? She only chuckled and said:

"I see something on her mast-head that will do for her!"

And whatever do you think it was she saw? It was the Devil in the form of a cat perched on the truck of the main mast.

"Leave it to him," said the old spae-wife, "leave it to him," and she chuckled again, most horrible to hear.

But meantime the Pageant is streaming past: trading ships, frigates, cutters and schooners, yawls and fishing-skiffs. And here come the steam-boats! That funny old tub with a funnel like a black chimney-stalk, and her big splashing wheels for paddles, is the S.S. *Helensburgh*, which, in August, 1825, was the first steamer to make a trip to Arran. That chubby steamboat is the *Toward Castle*, which an old advertisement in 1829 tells us sailed every Tuesday from the Broomielaw for Brodick and Lamlash, getting back on Wednesday. Beside it puffs the *Inveraray Castle,* which did the same adventurous voyage on Saturdays, and returned to Glasgow on the Monday. These lead the pageant of steam-boats, and after them come the *Hero* and the *Jupiter* and the *Juno,* Arran steamers between 1832 and 1864, and the *Earl of Arran* and the *Lady Mary* and the *Heather Bell* and the *Rothesay Castle* and the *Brodick Castle* and the *Ivanhoe* (sweetest of them all!) and the *Eagle* and the *Scotia* and the *Duchess of Hamilton* and the *Glen Sannox* and the *Atalanta.*

And now the rear-guard of the Pageant looms up, like huge citadels of grey, towering above the sea and smoking at their cones like floating volcanoes—cruisers and battleships that melted out of Lamlash Bay in August, 1914, and chased the German Eagle from all the Seven Seas, so that nowhere in them all was the black bird to be found.

When we have seen the splendid show sail past, don't you think we might call our island "Arran of the Ships"? From the very first age, that misty time when the log canoes first came in at Blackwaterfoot and Lagg, the folk of Arran have been great men of the sea, daring adventurers in little boats, in big boats, in skiffs that hunted the haddock with St. Peter's finger and thumb marks upon them and the fine sweet whiting and the flaky cod, in luggers with a smell of French brandy about them or white with smuggled salt, in ships that dodged the King's ships, in frigates that were the pride of the King's Navee. Aye, many a good tar the King got out of Arran, whether willingly or no. When an Arran man wanted to be a soldier, he nearly always joined the navy: that's a queer way of putting it, but you know what I mean. In the old days, before the Great War, there was a proverb which said, "There are two things no man has ever seen: the one is the death of a cadger's pony and the other is an Arran soldier." That was a joke, of course, for great and good soldiers came from Arran, like Colonel James Fullarton, who commanded the 96th Foot and who with other Arran men was through Corunna and Waterloo, and his brother, Major Archibald Fullarton, who fought in the Peninsula. Still the joke had a real edge to it once! The Great War has blunted the edge of it for ever, for no region in Auld Scotland gave more fully of its youth, or showed a finer courage or a brighter devotion in the battlefields afar as well as on the thundering seas, than Arran of the glens, the bens, and the brave. Yet in olden days it was the blue jacket more than the red coat that took the eye of the Arran lad who would be off in arms. Many a captain on his quarter-deck looked on his sea-dogs forward and counted on none so much for discipline and sobriety and bull-dog courage as the lads from our island clachans. More than one of these same lads came to walk his own poop as captain of a King's ship of the line. You will have heard of the M'Kirdys, uncle and nephew, it may be? Uncle M'Kirdy was a smuggler once, and gave fight one day to a revenue sloop that tried to round him up. Yes, and he defeated the King's ship, he did! Then a reward of £500 was put up for his capture. But what should the bold smuggler do but turn up himself and demand the reward. This made the captains and admirals scratch their heads, for clearly it was their duty to shoot the rascal, with the £500 in his pocket and all! But no, they couldn't do that. So they shipped him off in a frigate as bluejacket, and a fine one he made, for in time he got his commission and then command of a frigate man-o'-war. And boldly he carried the good ship through many a fight till, one fine day, he captured a French war-ship, running up to her and flinging the irons, and boarding her with pistols and cutlasses. But the Frenchmen, plucky fellows too, fired the magazine and up she blew and Captain M'Kirdy and the rest were killed in the explosion.

His nephew joined the navy, and worked before the mast till he became bo'sn of the ship. One night when the British fleet lay off the coast of France at Boulogne, watching the great Napoleon in case he should try to bring across to England the great army he had gathered in the camps on the green hills above that sandy shore, young M'Kirdy was sent in through the fog in a boat to reconnoitre. Coming back, he and his crew passed near a French frigate, and, seeing little sign of a guard on her, they slipped alongside, climbed like cats over the side, and were on the foe before you could say Jack Robinson—whatever the French for that may be! Quick as cats, they overcame the watch and then battened down the crew below. They sailed her away, a fine prize indeed, and M'Kirdy was given officer's rank, and some time after he too, like his uncle before him, got command of a frigate. Jolly good work!

I don't suppose Captain M'Kirdy, the uncle, was thought much more of in Arran, when he wore gold braid to his coat, than he was as a smuggler in a faded blue jersey. Smugglers, in Arran as elsewhere, were not looked upon as bad men, by any means. Even though the Law said, "Thou shalt not smuggle," people said, "It's a most unfair law and a nuisance besides to all honest men," and in spite of pains and penalties, they went on smuggling with quite a good conscience themselves, and a quiet respect for all who did the same, especially for those who did it bravely and successfully. To understand this, you must know that taxes then were heavy, and some of them ridiculously unfair. The Government was hard up for money to carry on the wars of the Continent, and so up went the old taxes and up went new taxes, taxes on malt and wines and salt and whisky. Ships came from France with wine, you see, and had a thumping big duty to pay on being landed in Scotland. So on dark nights the ships would steer a course near Arran and send the barrels ashore, where the smugglers hid them, and afterwards took them over in smacks to Ayrshire, and so smuggled them in. Salt too was brought in thus. Do you know that the tax on salt was so heavy that it raised the price of it to forty times its original cost? Then, there was whisky. At one time any man could distil whisky just as he pleased. But the Government stepped in and said, "You must have a licence for making whisky." It was difficult to get a licence, and besides it cost money, and, more than that, it was interfering with the freedom which the people had had since that great teetotal time, the Flood. For other reasons as well, the folk of Arran thought it no wrong to have sma' stills in a good hiding-place in the lonely burn or along the desert shore, and no wrong either in doing anything and everything to hoodwink the men of the Excise as they darted here and there through the island, or patrolled the coast in their revenue cutters.

The smugglers were of two kinds, although often a man was both. There were the smugglers who made whisky secretly, and there were the smugglers who got it and the rest past the island or out of the island and across to the mainland, without the Customs folk getting at it to tax it. Many a secret place in the glens can the old folk tell you of, where the stills bubbled and the white whisky flowed, and many a cave on the shore where the kegs were stowed, and many a cove from which on mirky nights and in boisterous seas the smugglers' boats put in and out. Many a fight besides there was between the grim lads with the kegs and the men of the Excise hovering like hawks about, and men were shot dead, or taken and tried in Edinburgh and shipped away as convicts to the West Indies; and the King's men were beaten back with oars, or pistolled as they came aboard, and driven off, swearing they would make the smugglers pay dearly for this!

Thus it was one October evening between Pladda and Kildonan, that the King's cutter, the *Prince Augustus Frederick* ran across the bows of a salt smuggler there, and called her to heave to in the King's name. But the men rose up, and, lifting the oars, thrust and smote at the excisemen, and many a clour they dealt them. Up went a pistol in the boat, the shot rang out and down fell a lad in the boat stone dead. That sobered them all and the boat was taken.

Thus it was, too, in 1817, on March 27, that

smugglers set out from the south of Arran with whisky aboard. Quietly they set sail, and gently they laid a course for Ayrshire, when what should they see but a revenue cutter nosing her way round the point, and bearing across to cut them off. Down went the tiller, up came the smack in the wind, round she fluttered, in drew the sheets, and over she heeled on her way to the shore again. But the cutter had seen it all, and, shifting another point off the wind, she ran down to get between the smack and the beach. Getting into stays, she lowered a boat, and ten men well-armed jumped in. "Give way!" cried the officer in charge; the oars bent like willows, and off she surged to the landing-place. The smugglers got there first, beaching the smack at full sail, and, leaping out, heaved the kegs ashore, and, tumbling out after them, began to carry the precious stuff on their broad backs up the shore. They had got some way when their pursuers overtook them. Down bumped the kegs on the grass, dour and desperate stood the smugglers in the circle of their foes, but they were outnumbered, and kept their hands to themselves. So the revenue men seized the kegs, and, hoisting them up, began to carry them off to their boat, with many a hard jest at the others' defeat. But all this had not gone unnoticed by the folk in the cottages near by. Out came men and women with glum faces and anger smouldering in their eyes; down they moved to the shore and the victorious sailors, about them they closed, crying, "Shame to you, ye robbers of poor folk!" and "Lay down the stuff of these honest lads!" Then from crying out such words, they took to jostling the sailors, and from jostling, they passed to laying hands on the kegs and on those carrying them, and in a flash the fight began! The officer, whose name was John Jeffrey, appealed to the folk to keep clear or take the consequences. He pled with them to stand away and not hinder the doing of his duty. But blood was up by now, bitter blows were struck, men grappled with one another and rolled wrestling on the ground, lads had excisemen by the throat, women came skirmishing around, shrieking loudly and dealing fell wounds with their nails, when at last Jeffrey ordered his men to fire. Out blazed the shots, and when the smoke cleared, there on the ground lay two men and a woman writhing in the throes of death. M'Kinnon was the name of the men, and the woman was Isabel Nichol. With that woe, blood cooled and the parties drew off from each other. But the wailing for the dead reached as far as Edinburgh, for Jeffrey was put on trial there for manslaughter, but judged "Not Guilty," as it was held by the judge that he had only done his duty in commanding his men to fire.

SHIPS AND SMUGGLERS: THE STORY

SHIPS AND SMUGGLERS: THE STORY

"The Tale of Dan Cook of Largie Beg"

OLD DONALD took the old clay pipe from between his old blue lips, and, after a proper pause, spat well forward on the ground. The old white hen, who would never learn wisdom, looked and hobbled away with disgust and disappointment glaring in her old eyes.

Donald and I were sitting on a wooden bench which leaned crazily against the wall of that cottage of his in A., which was partly dwelling-house and partly a shop where, according to the sign written above the door in frail blue letters, "General Provisions" was "lisenced to sell Tabaco." I was a lad of fifteen then, and on that particular August day had been dispatched on a venturesome effort to persuade old Donald's wife to sell us a pot of jam. The effort failed. What was wanted above all else was a pot of black-currant jam, and Kirsty (the only name by which we knew Donald's wife) said that aye certainly indeed there would be a pot of black currants somewhere, and that she would be finding it! Up she climbed on a stool to reach the shelf where the little fat jars stood in rows, each with its paper cover gummed round its neck like a frill. Not all of these had their names scrawled on the top in ink the colour of honey, and of those that had them none had the title required. So Kirsty had to jab a wrinkled finger through the tight parchment of several, and drew it out smeared with the dark sweet stuff, which she tasted, smacking her lips and pondering the flavour with her head to one side. The last of these was Black Currant, indeed it was, to be sure, but Kirsty said:

"Well, well, it is indeed the black currants, but you won't be able to buy it. It is the grand thing for the cold and a sore throat too, and you'll be seeing it is the last one at all!"

So we came to terms on a pot of wild raspberry jam, and Kirsty began the slow work of mending the holes in the broken covers with patches torn from yesterday's *Glasgow Herald,* and stuck around with the selvidge of postage stamps.

Outside, old Donald was sunning himself on the bench, watching the hens as they still found something to peck at among the white gravel and the lawn of tired grass beyond, or screwing up his eyes to look beyond the reddening rowan trees and the corn fields and the yellow sand of the shore, and watch the *Duchess of Hamilton* crossing the blue bay, stately and queenly as a duke's lady.

He was ready for a crack even with a schoolboy, and many a tale he told as he sat there in the sun, seeing all old things clearly in that evening light of age, which is the gift of old men.

"Well I remember," he said that morning, "when there was no steamboats whatever coming into Whiting Bay but only to Lamlash, and nothing but fishing-boats and the big smack that was sailing from Glen Ashdale to Ardrossan and maybe to Ayr at times too. Aye, aye, well, well!"

"There would be luggers too, Donald," said I in the pause that followed.

"Certainly there was luggers; and what will you mean by luggers?" he replied.

"O luggers, you know!" I explained as boys do by simply repeating what they said before. "Luggers, you know: smugglers' boats and revenue cutters chasing them, and fights on the shore and in caves between the excisemen and the smugglers, you know!"

"Smugglers it is," the old man answered. "O yes, now and then there was smugglers here and there, they'll be telling me, but that was long ago. You wouldn't be thinking I was a smuggler, would you now?"

And Donald chuckled in a way that raised a most hopeful suspicion in my mind: but in vain.

"O yes, yes, there was smugglers now and then, they'll be telling me," continued Donald. "Fine I could show you a place in the burn yonder and a few more forbye, where they would be having the sma' stills hidden away just neat. Aye, and a good place in Holy Isle, and a good place at Largie Beg, where the skiffs sailed away at night with the good stuff aboard, yes indeed."

"Largie Beg, Donald!" I interrupted. "Did you ever hear tell of a smuggler at Largie Beg, who tied up a revenue man and then cut his throat?"

"Hoots away with you!" said Donald, sharply; "who's been telling you the havers? It never was: but it was Dan Cook at Largie Beg [36] who had the great to-do with the King's men at Largie Beg, and the people were laughing from Bennan to Brodick about it after. O, he was the lad was Dan Cook, a big man with a long nose, and he was always sniffing when he was talking, and 'Who are you to set yourself up?' it would be sounding like. He was amusing!"

Donald by now was well under way, and thus I got the tale of Dan Cook at Largie Beg.

It was indeed at Largie Beg that Dan Cook was living, him and his wife, and she was the brave woman too. There they would be all alone, but the wee herd lad for the two cows or maybe three or four. It is a good house, and it is standing there as before with everything else. Aye, and from the door you will look that way and there is the bay between you and the Dippen Rocks to the southart, and you will look this way, and there is the bay past Largie Meanach to Largie Mor at the Black Rocks.

Well, well, do you know it was in the burn there in the Dippen Bay, and it was very near to the house, that Dan had his sma' still working away and him making good stuff, and getting good money over the water when he would sail in his skiff to Saltcoats or somewhere, I am not sure. It was working away a long time it was, that wee still, after the others about the burns there was all caught and carried away by the revenue folk. But there you are, they couldn't find Dan's still: ah, he was the amusing lad!

You see, he was born there, and every rock and hole and every cave on the shore he knew as well as you could, and he had one cave down below, and it was all thick with brackens and whins and brambles too, likely, and wouldn't he carry his still down there to hide it every time indeed that the gaugers came about like ferrets along a dyke? He was the lad, Dan, as strong as the big red stag that John Hamilton killed up the Glen, when he carried away on its horns his high fence he built to keep them out of his corn. You see it was against the law indeed to lay a hand on the deer, or to kill them what is more, but was it against the law for them to let deer to grow like that stag on poor man's corn, will you tell me that? The law—— . . . Aye, aye, well, well, it was about Dan Cook: I'm not forgetting! . . . Well now, they couldn't be nabbing him at all, at his wee still, and there he was laughing and sniffing away and doing fine. But the neighbours would say, "They'll be catching ye yet, Dan lad!" And the minister himself from Kilmorie came away in by, and he had his suspicions of Dan, and knew about it all as well as the rest; and the minister took his bit dram in Dan's house and said, with a look in his eye, "Aye, aye, Dan, there is no question in the Catechism about whisky at all," and Dan would laugh and see the minister up to the road, and Dan would be going to the church that Sabbath and maybe one more running.

Well, the time went on, and there was people born and there was people buried, and all the while there was Dan working away. But one day, they'll be saying, along the road came Alastair Stewart from Kiscadale over there; he had a funeral for the day of his cousin at Dippen going to Kilmorie. And there was Dan looking over the wall and smoking and looking at nothing. And Alastair stopped and took off his hat and he wiped away at his face, it being a warm day and him with his black clothes on him, with a crepe round about his hat, and a hard collar to his neck.

"Well, well," says Alastair, "and you'll be knowing that the cutter is sailing at Loch-an-Eilean the day, Dan?"

"Indeed," says Dan, with a face as innocent as you could see. "Indeed," says he, "and what business will that be to me, Alastair Stewart?"

"O none at all, none at all," says Alastair, quite serious; "none at all, none at all; but she's a good boat, and I thought maybe you'd like to be calling to them when they sail by to come in by and rest a bit."

So they cracked away together, and then Alastair put back his hat on his head, for he would be going now to the funeral of his cousin from Dippen to Kilmorie, and away he went up the road. But Dan put his pipe away in his waistcoat pouch and took a dauner to the front of the brae and looked away to Largie Mor, and I declare to my goodness, what did he see but the revenue boat coming along with a north wind from King's Cross Point, and he didn't like to see the way she was heading. Dan rubbed his hand down his nose, and thought a while, and then he said, "Imphm aye, it's just possible!" and with that he called to Jeanie his wife, for that was her name, and says he, "Jeanie woman, there's a bird coming; we'd be better to get the worm put out of sight from her," meaning, to be sure, the sma' still. O he was the amusing lad, was Dan Cook. Jeanie said nothing—she was the business-like wife for a man—and the two of them together went down to the burn, and away they took the wee still between them out from the brackens, and over the stones and down the hill as quick as you could, and to the shore and into the cave which they knew, and well hidden it was, as well that you couldn't guess even if you were pulling brambles at the very mouth of it. O she was the powerful woman, a real help-meet for an honest man! My old grandmother was telling me long ago about Jeanie M'Kelvie, that was Dan Cook's wife, that once she was so strong that she took a stirk by the head that came into the byre, and what do you think she did——

. . . Very well, I'll tell you another time, as you say, but she was the powerful woman. The stirk——

. . . Very good, I'm not forgetting about the cutter, but you mustn't hurry a man with his story. Well, well, up the brae comes Dan and Jeanie, and they got to the house well and good, when what was it at the bay at Largie Meanach but the cutter putting a boat ashore with three men in her, and two of them stepped ashore and left a man to mind the boat, and up the two were coming to the houses at Largie Beg. When Dan caught sight of this, he sent Jeanie away to a neighbour's and into the house he went. But before that, round to the byre he goes and gets a couple of two pitch-forks for the hay and in he brings them to the house, with an end of rope besides; and he ties the two ends of the pitch-forks together with the rope, making a lashing of them together, for that was a bit of his ploy, as I'm telling you. And there he was in the lobby between the two doors of the house that runs from the front door to the back door, and he kept the two doors shut, and he stood in the middle with the points of the hay-forks holding them behind the doors. He was the clever lad, Dan!

Well and now, up comes the two gaugers, very very smart men by their way of thinking it, and the one went to the front door, and the other took a turn round the house to the back door, and there they cried, "Open, Dan Cook, in the King's name!" But all that Dan would do was to laugh and say, "Open the door yourself for a change, and just you come in ben!" So they pushed at the doors, and nearly ran their noses on the hay-forks, and they stopped and they saw that here was trouble. But Dan said, "Ach now, you're surely not changing your minds to have a bite of dinner here this day! I'll just be letting you have the tooth-picks before you come to the mutton, like!" But would they come in? No: they thought twice about it, I'm telling you, and round came the one at the back door and had a talk with his mate, and the one waited to keep Dan there, and the other went away in a hurry to get more assistance from the cutter. When what do you think Dan will be up to next, but he is out of the house like a collie over a dyke, and grips the one at the door like a dog with a rat, and shakes him till the teeth of him shook in his head with a clatter, and down he got him, and along he pulled him by the scruff of his neck, and then tied him like a sheep hand and foot, and lifted him like a bairn and put him away into a hole in the peat-stack, and built up a wall of divots to keep him snug and warm like! O he was the wonder, was Dan. Aye, aye, and into the house he gets himself in good time too, before the men from the cutter comes up. Did I tell you that the man from the back door would be away to get help from the cutter?

Well, he did, and the skipper of her swore like a trooper in Ayr, and orders his men to take guns and pistols and cutlasses, and be quick about it, and up the shore at Largie Meanach they came in a duvvle of a hurry—I mean truly speedily that is, and up to Dan's house with their sea-legs out of breath. Then up speaks the skipper and says:

"Surrender in the King's name!"

Dan all this while was behind the door for

"Tied him like a sheep, hand and foot."—P. 232.

certain, and they could hear him give a sniff, and then he cried out:

"Away with you and not be troubling me when I want to have a bit snooze this warm day!"

The skipper looked round to see if any of his men was laughing up his sleeve, for they knew Dan, some of them did, to be the wag he was, and then he cried:

"Dan Cook, in the King's name, give yourself up, and be slippy about it!"

But Dan would do no such thing, but he cried:

"I have two cocks as it is: away and find a dung-hill for yourself and learn to crow yonder, auld claret face!"

This gave the skipper a flea in his lug, and up he gets and orders his men to fire a volley of their guns over the house. My faith, it was a noise they made, there is no mistake! They was telling that the sound of it was heard at Dippen, and the minister stopped in his prayer at Alastair Stewart's funeral for his cousin, and old Mary Currie, Alastair's good-sister, fell with a skreich on the floor, and broke all the glasses for the dram they would be having before they started away for Kilmorie. And all the collies at Largie Beg ran away yowling to Largie Mor, and the kye put up their tails and went off to the moor, and the hens flew over the house, and the big sow caught the wee herd lad and cowpit him into the water of the dung-hill. And lo and behold, there was Dan standing at the door as neat and cool as a pat of butter on a cabbage leaf, and looking round him calm as a judge.

"Goodness gracious, I declare," says Dan, "what was that noise whatever? Has the French landed?"

Then up comes the skipper, swearing so bad that Dan put his fingers in his ears to keep it out, and he says:

"Look you, Cook, where is my man? What have you been doing with him?"

And Dan says, with a face of innocence, "Your man? I've not lost a man. Count your men for yourself. I'm no great hand at the counting."

"You blackguard!" cries the skipper, and he turns to his men and says, "Off with you, men, and find him!"

Surely enough they began to hear a wailing and a crying like a bairn shut up in a meal chest, and this was the man in the peat-stack wailing, for he heard the guns fire and knew that here was his friends at last.

Well, off they went, and off went Dan alongside, rubbing his nose with his hand and sniffing away, and he would be saying:

"Do you hear a crying now? Glory to goodness, was your sailors killing my pig? By gum," he would say, "if your sailors was killing my pig, my bonny wee pig, I'll have the price of her in your blood, I will!"

In time they come to the peat-stack, and there he was, and very like a pig in a stye too, I'll be thinking. Out he is pulled, and the rope gets cut at once, and everybody turns to Dan and fair scowls at him. But Dan holds up his hands like an old wife at another old wife's story, and says he:

"Did you ever! How did the lad get into the peats? Maybe he wanted a place to smoke, and maybe he would be setting the stack on fire with his smoking, the scoundrel!"

"*You* are the scoundrel, you long-nosed blackguard," cries the skipper, coming up to him. "It was you that set him there, you double-faced smuggler!"

But Dan would only be stroking his nose and saying:

"Isn't it the fair confusion how the lad got there? It is the fair wonder!"

And nothing more could they get out of Dan but the same, he standing and glowering at the peat-stack and the man, and back again to the hole in the divots. O he was the amusing lad, Dan.

Ach well, it was the finest thing for all the neighbours who were there, holding their hands across their mouths and saying to Dan, "It would be the Wee Folk that did it on the man, Dan!" and Dan would say, "Maybe Neil, maybe Jeanie, or maybe the Duvvle! They are uncanny lads the gaugers."

Well, well, they scattered and looked for the wee sma' still, but ach, they would be looking for a needle in a hay-rick, the callans, and they peched away about the brackens at the burn and beneath stones and rocks, and behind the whins, and down to the shore, but never a smell of it they had.

So surely, the skipper blew a whistle and away they would go to their boats! And Dan walked down behind them a bit of the road, with his hands in his belt, and whistling for a tune "The Devil caught the Gauger": aye, and a very good piper he was, was Dan in the evenings on the roadside at Largie Beg. And the skipper said to him, What was he following for? And Dan said:

"I was keeping an eye on the lad that was smoking in yon peat-stack. I wouldn't wonder if he was after my divots to light his fire on your bonny bit boat!"

But then Dan came back to the folk at his house, and they laughed and slapped him on his back. All that they could get Dan to be saying was this and no more:

"Ach, isn't it a great amusement, the gauger lads? But it is indeed a bit of a nuisance too, whatever!"

O he was the fair divert, was Dan Cook!

REFERENCES ON MAP

Number on Map	Description of Site	Page References
1	Fort: Torr an t-Sean Chaisteil, ...	15, 101
2	North Sannox Cairn (Cist), ...	28
3	Site of Circle, ...	
4	Fragments of large Cairn, ...	24
5	Chapel site, ...	63
6	Cairn ("Sannox Chamber"), ...	23
7	Merkland Point Cist, ...	28
8	Standing Stones (Deer Park), ..	28
9	Standing Stone (Stronach), ...	28
10	Standing Stone, ...	28
11	Cup and Ring Rocks, ...	
12	Cairn, ...	24
13	Cairn ("Columba's Resting-place"),	24
14	Standing Stone (East Mayish), ...	28
15	Glencloy Chapel, ...	63
16	Cairn (Glenrickard Chamber), ...	24
17	Fort: Torr an t-Sean Chaisteil, ...	15, 101, 152, 164
18	Fort: Dun Fionn, ...	15, 19, 102
19	Stone Circle and Cist, ...	27
20	Dun Mor, ...	23
21	Dun Beg (and Standing Stone), ...	23
22	Standing Stones, ...	28, 183
23	Chapel of Kilbride, ...	61
24	Ruins of Monastery, ...	53, 67
25	Cave of St. Molaise: Judgment Stone, ...	15, 54, 70, 99
26	Benlister Cist, ...	28
27	Glenkil Cist, ...	27
28	Cairn: (south above Monamor Burn),	24
29	Viking's Grave, King's Cross, ...	15, 103
30	Fort, King's Cross, ...	102
31	Achancairn Cairn, ...	27
31A	Cnocan a'Choilich Cist, ...	27, 36
32	Glenashdale Fort, ...	34, 102
33	Remains of Chapel, ...	63
34	The Giant's Grave and small Cairn,	14, 20, 29, 41
35	Stone Circle above Largie Beg, ...	28
36	Remains of Circle with Cist, Largie Beg, ...	15, 28, 226
37	Ballymeanach Chamber, ...	24
38	Cairn (Dippen), ...	24
39	Dippen Greenhill Cist, ...	28
40	Fort, ...	100
41	Remains of Chapel, ...	61
42	Kildonan Castle, ...	134
43	Stone Circle, Kildonan, ...	28

INDEX

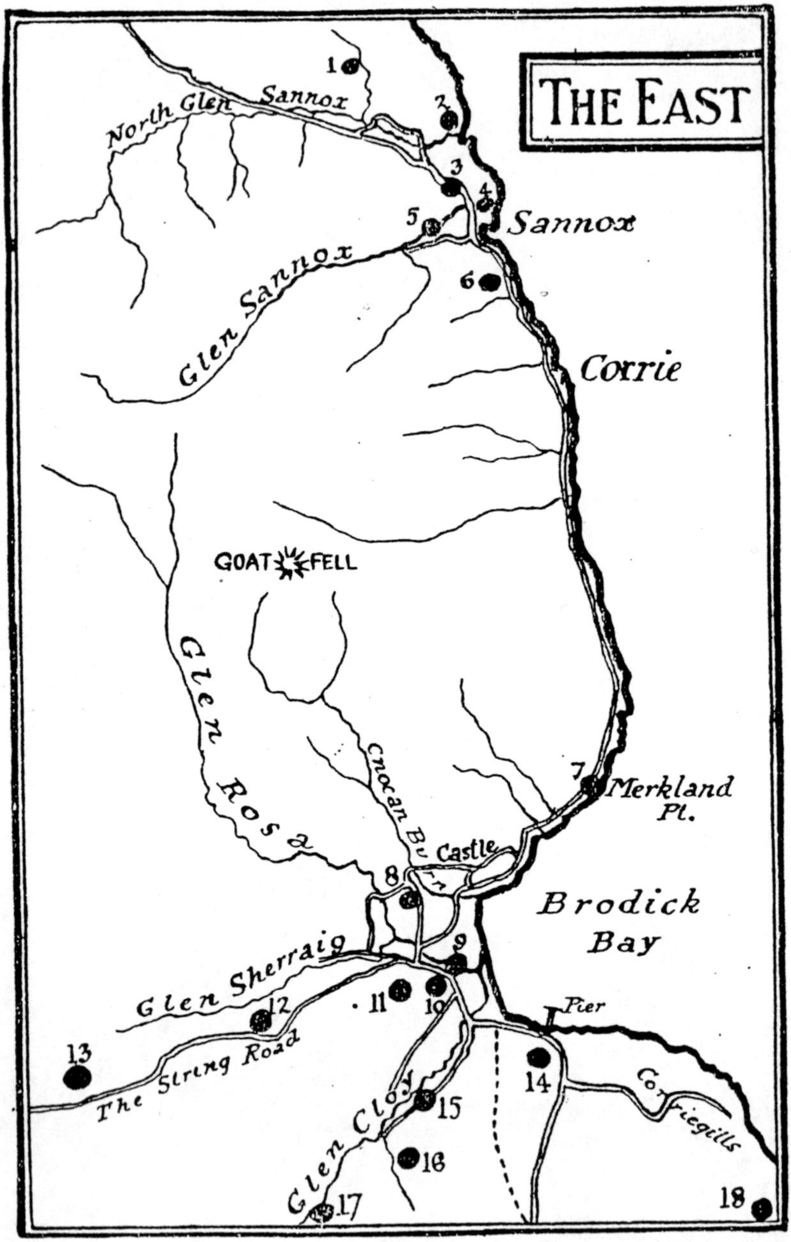
THE EAST
North Glen Sannox
Sannox
Glen Sannox
Corrie
GOAT FELL
Glen Rosa
Cnocan Burn
Merkland Pt.
Castle
Brodick Bay
Glen Sherraig
Pier
The String Road
Glen Cloy
Corriegills
1
2
3
4
5
6
7
8
9
10
11
12
13
14
15
16
17
18

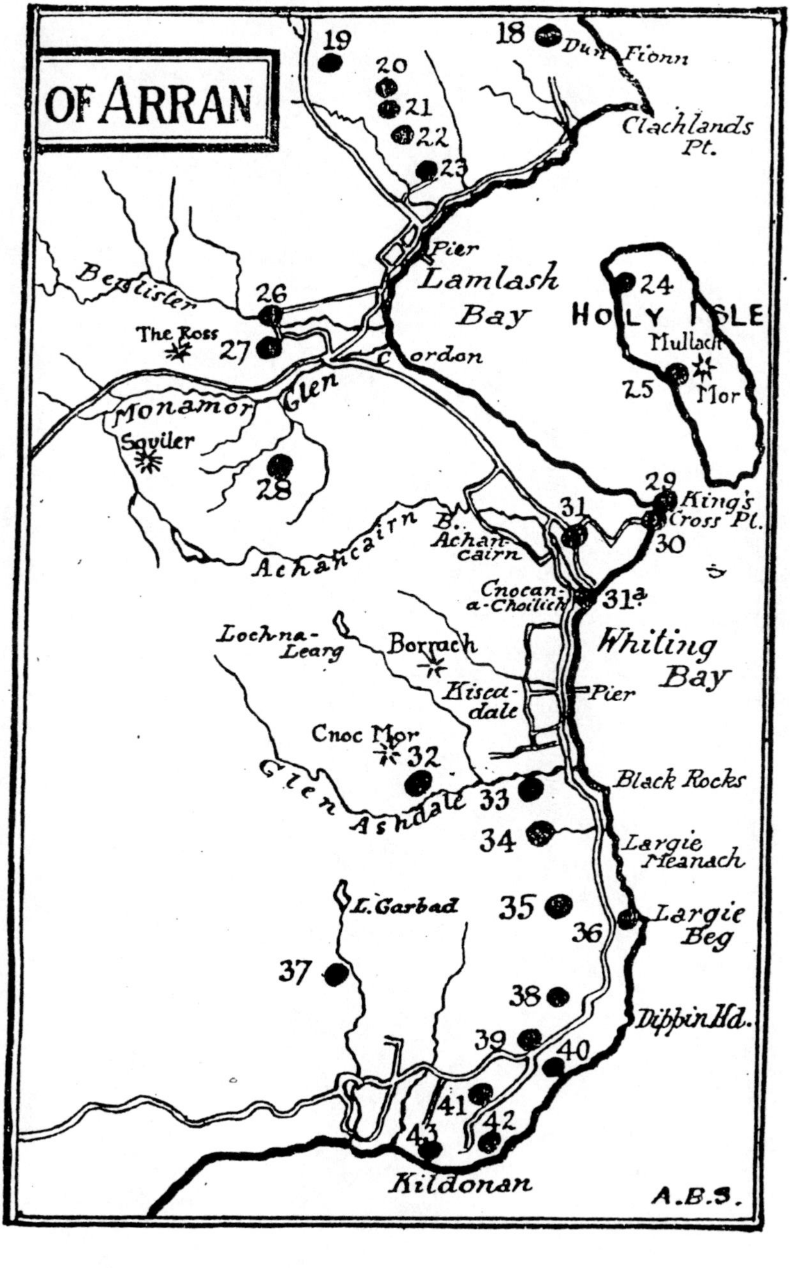
OF ARRAN
19
20
21
22
23
18
Dun Fionn
Clachlands Pt.
Pier
Lamlash Bay
24
HOLY ISLE
Mullach Mor
25
26
Benlister
The Ross
27
Cordon
Monamor Glen
Sgriler
28
29
King's Cross Pt.
30
31
B. Achancairn
Achancairn
Cnocan-a-Choilich
31a
Loch-na-Learg
Borrach
Whiting Bay
Kiscadale
Pier
Cnoc Mor
32
Glen Ashdale
33
Black Rocks
34
Largie Meanach
35
L. Garbad
36
Largie Beg
37
38
Dippin Hd.
39
40
41
42
43
Kildonan
A.B.S.